THE CLICHÉ

Michael A. Occhionero

AOS Publishing, 2024
Copyright © 2024

Michael A. Occhionero

All rights reserved under International
and Pan-American copyright conventions

ISBN: 978-1-990496-80-6

Cover Design: Ariel Lacombe

Visit AOS Publishing's website:
www.aospublishing.com

"You know,

I've heard the term thrown around quite a bit on the television lately. Come to think of it, I've also seen it in books a few times. Every time I hear or read it, I smile and nod and act like I know exactly what is going on, like I'm hip to the joke, when truly I'm just an old washed-up rancher who hasn't a gosh darn clue what the world is onto these days. What's even nuttier? Despite that wicked fast portable gizmo always in my pocket, shrinking my genitals with its X- or UV- or whatever-kinda rays, and despite the digital encyclopedia it's got, holding a greater mass of human knowledge than the burnt-up Library of Alexandria (not to mention a whole Pandora's box of other diversions), I never reckoned to look it up. Them city slickers call it one small step for man, and one huge leap for humanity! No matter if the leap into cyberspace is a leap firmly away from God.

Mhm.

It's just like my grandpappy used to say: just 'cause you can answer a few questions, don't mean you're asking the right ones!' This was one of his favorite sayin's. Pappy'd just sit his big ol' haunch down in the creaky rockin' chair we had out on the porch with a fifth of rye, whittling his life away on those little cedar wood figurines. He was a nasty old bugger, and I liked buggin' him 'til he got real mad. Admittedly, I was a pain in the neck myssel, and I wouldn't quit 'til the old man'd up and chase me with his old leather strop! Oooo-eee, he was real intent on givin' me a whoopin'! Never did catch me, though, hehe. Grandpappy'd always collapse before he ever made it off the porch. Blamed it on the old age. I always reckoned the rye mighta had a lil' somethin' to do with it. But you can't account for a man's pride. The old man dropped in '74. I was sixteen, or thereabouts, and it took all of me not to cry at the bastard's funeral. God bless him. So, I guess what I'm asking is, in layman's terms, if you would, might'n you tell me just what in the hell the word 'Postmodernism' means?"

—Jimbo Delacroix, sixty-three years of age, staunch Christian, beloved husband and rhetorical, non-recurring one-off

Wowie, well howdy there Jimbo! Ain't we super glad you asked! That's so *funny*, you know? We were floating around in a café the other day, and we overheard a couple of turtle-necked art students talking about this mysterious 'Postmodernism'. And now, only a few eternities later, you're asking about it! Isn't that wild?

Gee, don't those kinds of coincidences, or providences (*wink wink*) just give you shivers sometimes? It's almost like it all *has to* mean something, like there *has to* be someone or something out there pulling the strings, keeping the whole simulation afloat!

But now, let us get serious and try to answer your question as succinctly as we can.

Postmodernism, first and foremost, designates a period in history. However, it is also an artistic movement or school of thought, which in some slippery way has evolved into a sort of socio-political stance that some might even call a worldview.

Let's start with the history.

According to scholars, the period known as Postmodern began in the post-war 1950's. Some even think that the Postmodern period has bled into the present one, overlapping with the onset of the Information Age.

Early Postmodernism was marked by the horrors of World War II, as well as by the growing skepticism of God that followed in their wake. Consequently, this period produced a large swathe of scholars, critics, and artists whose faith in history and humankind had been deeply, deeply shaken. This shaken faith provoked a growing skepticism of what were coined the 'Master' or 'Meta Narratives', these being the narratives that had, historically, been used to justify cultural practices, norms, and traditions. These 'Meta Narratives', or alternatively, the grand stories that humans had passed down for generations in an attempt to retain links to their past and make sense of who they were, the Postmodernists insisted, were subjective. And by virtue of that subjectivity, they were nothing but spin. In fact, since everything was a story invented by humans, nothing was ever anything but spin. History, the Postmodernists deduced, by nature of being 'His' story, was little more than a fictional narrative told by the powerful (usually white and male) to keep the weak or marginalized (highlight females, ethnic minorities, and/or non-heterosexuals) under their thumb. Consequently, those traditionally in control of these 'Master Narratives', these 'choice few', gained undue, and indeed often oppressive control over the others merely subjected to their undeniable influence. Those in control – the 'oppressors' – did all they could to perpetuate the status quo that kept them in control. Whereas the marginalized, victimized groups on the B-side of the universal power struggle had absolutely no recourse to change. This, of course, was unfair. And so, the Postmodernists concluded, the entire capitalist system and all the institutions it spawned were inherently evil. And as evil, they needed to be radically reformed, if not entirely destroyed.

As a critical movement, Postmodernism became popular especially for the advent of 'Deconstructionism' in literary theory, and for Jacques Derrida's famously controversial axiom: 'There is no outside-text'. Though scholarly proponents of Derrida might resist the prevalent, though simplified interpretation of this famous quote, there are also many who insist that Derrida's statement posits the following logical track: since all thought is language, and all language is constructed by human beings, all thought is, like human beings, relative and subjective. Thus, since knowledge is always conferred through subjective language, it follows logically that there can be no universal, or Meta-truth (thus equally, causally, inevitably, no God). Perhaps as famous as Derrida's morbidly misinterpreted mantra is critic Michel Foucault's societal analogy of the 'Panopticon', which is based on Jeremy Bentham's revolutionary eighteenth century jail design of the same name – a circular surveillance scheme in which every prisoner held in the Panopticon could be surveilled by a single guard in the center of the structure, without the prisoners being able to tell at any time whether or not they were being watched (in modern terms, one might think of covert state surveillance, or even of something as innocuous as targeted marketing, wherein a Ping-Pong table casually mentioned in conversation mysteriously becomes the first ad one sees upon opening their favorite social media application, for example).

Following its critical dictates, Postmodern art, and especially Postmodern literature, often finds itself 'breaking the fourth wall', and so acknowledging itself as art (think of it this way: every time we talk to you, you remember you're reading a book). Postmodern art often makes use of intertextuality (overt references to other texts or pieces of art, sharing and affirming the art you're consuming's status as art), practicing self-reflexivity and self-analysis (Hello!), striving to make its reader or viewer uncomfortable (Care to see a dick pic?) and ultimately succumbing to neurosis (Hello again, we were just kidding about the dick pic, we promise! Please don't go!). Postmodern art resists straightforward interpretation, and insists that the creative process is paramount to the final result. Postmodern art tends to be avant-garde, markedly anti-bourgeois, subversive, and oftentimes deliberately obscure. Colored by its rejection of universal truth, it naturally would not attempt to convince the reader or viewer of its reality or objectivity, but would instead acknowledge its status as subjective art, effectively blurring the lines between fact and fiction.

As a worldview, or 'condition', the Postmodern is often linked to the progressive, the political left, and the contemporary. Postmodernists maintain close scholarly and political ties with Marxists, proponents of Political Correctness, Feminists, and Gender Theorists. They often subscribe to the overarching notions of socially constructed identities based on the fluidity of knowledge, truth, and sexuality. Postmodern thinkers often distrust contemporary information societies that aim to control identity through image and narrative making. Postmodernism is very much a doctrine of the metropolis, where tyrannical, patriarchal hierarchies are more forthrightly realized, causing the marginalized to endure a constant power struggle against those with access to privileged positions within the 'Master Narratives' of the Patriarchy. The Postmodern creed that all language is metaphor precludes the possibility for literal truth. Thus, even sciences like Psychology and Biology cannot be trusted, because they are contaminated by the foolish fallacy of objectivity. Reason itself is tyrannical, as it marginalizes emotion. Because language is thought, the control of discourse equates to the wielding of power, which means that speech itself can at times be violence. Furthermore, according to the Postmodernists the individual is not sovereign, but is rather the product or epiphenomenon of the discourse surrounding his or her group identity as fitted within the larger hierarchy (as demonstrated by the popular assertion that all straight white males are necessarily privileged via their participation and support of evil patriarchal systems of discourse). The Postmodern worldview encourages pluralism, and diversity, not the rigidity of oppositions or binaries. The Postmodernists assert that the dissolution of unifying frameworks is the only way to eliminate marginalization. In other words, centralization (people coming together) results in power being unevenly distributed, and so is inherently *problematic.*

Critics of Postmodernism often point out that the pessimism, deconstruction, and social criticisms of Postmodernists have yet to be counterbalanced with an optimistic attempt at a solution. In other words, while Postmodernists make for excellent deconstructors, they, as of yet, are inadequate constructors.

And one final point:

The Postmodern Condition, as it has evolved into the Information Age, is marked by the particular contemporary phenomenon that is the sensory overload of images facilitated by the instant access to entertainment (or distraction), which leaves the individual identity in a constant state of seeking, dissatisfaction, and flux that absolutely obliterates any and all notions of stability of character and continuity through time. The mental effects of this phenomenon of fluidity, of course, are only just beginning to materialize.

"All are called, but in any given generation few are chosen, because few choose themselves."

-- Aldous Huxley, *The Perennial Philosophy* (1945)

"To Love and Be Wise is Impossible."

-- Spanish Proverb found in a Perugina Baci chocolate
a few days after Mao's breakup (2019)

"The thing about *my* two cents, though, is that it's worth at least a dollar."

\-- Mao, with a mouth full of Perugina Baci chocolate,
crumpled proverb in hand (2019)

"A book with four epigraphs is indeed a most ridiculous book."

-- Unknown (?)

I

Ah, here we are!

Finally!

We've been expecting you.

Please, sit down!

It's time to begin the story.

This story, dear reader, like many, many stories before it, begins in the dense fog of a struggling hero's psyche.

We don't mean any of that in the literal or conventional sense, of course. Language is a metaphorical device, and so you will excuse us if there is no actual fog. This story takes place in Montréal, not in London, and so the story's climate will mostly oscillate between the manic extremes of Montréal's very hot summers and excruciatingly cold winters. There is hardly ever fog in Montréal. The fog, dear and cherished reader, is a figurative stand-in for the muddled inner folds of our hero's mind.

That word again... hero.

To clarify, our hero won't be wielding any swords or shields.

No bows and arrows.

There will be no battling of any dragons... or any literal ones, anyway.

And yet a hero he is! Nonetheless.

This struggling hero has, one could say, an *unusual* name. One that not many others have. An unfortunate name, some might say. But then, one has little power over a parent's passing whim...

The hero's name is... well, it is Mao.

First of all, we know exactly what you're thinking, and you *aren't* clever for thinking it! Besides, that has nothing to do with it at all. Mao was not even Asian, let alone Chinese. He was not a communist, and he did not wield unseemly power over anyone or anything. Anyone or anything *real,* anyway. What he was, this so-called hero, was a twenty-seven-year-old cisgender, heterosexual, Caucasian, toxically oversexed male, raised Catholic (*very problematic*), with tertiary attributes like beautiful brown eyes, a big but not quite cartoonish nose, a nearly bald head, and an athletic physique softened by marijuana-induced eating binges that he shamefully, yet regularly succumbed to after dark. Oh, and despite the fact that he didn't wear glasses or have any tweed in his wardrobe, he fancied himself some sort of poet, or writer, or something. Yes, *seriously.* The moron spent hours and hours writing *books,* in his day and age. We know. *We know*! Books! What kind of masochist? Everyone knows that no one reads anymore!

In case it still needs clarifying, this was the year 2019 A.D on the planet Earth of the Milky Way galaxy.

Now, despite all that we've suffered to explain, and despite how much sense it all seems to make, one might still be thinking that the name 'Mao' is somewhat implausible.

Well, we say one probably needs to work on his or her or they or them's sense of humor!

Fine!

Alright!

You caught us.

We admit it!

The name Mao is obviously a fake.

We knew you'd be too shrewd to buy into something as obviously fake as that. You, after all, are the cream of the crop. You're one of the dwindling few who actually do read books in the age of the infinite scroll! But alright, relax. There's no need to get all puffed up and elitist. No one is that impressed. You can get your head out of your ass.

How's this: you could think of Mao as an acronym of sorts, if you're feeling particularly cheeky, or otherwise as an epithet for our hero's tyrannical tendencies.

No, no, no. We already told you that Mao was neither a political nor a radical. What he was, sweet reader, was an avid reader. He was well-read, and he enjoyed the work of both Ayn Rand *and* Karl Marx. Certainly, he did! Well, he enjoyed Marx more conceptually, you know? The old beggar's writing was actually rather frightful. Mao viewed the two as exponents of equally unlikely and diametrically opposed pipedreams that canceled out fairly neatly in the middle ground everyone (or mostly everyone, anyway) called reality. Aside from a six-week stint of his own puffed-up elitism inspired by his month-long journey through the deranged, monolithic masterpiece *Atlas Shrugged,* Mao was generally left-leaning, and usually voted Liberal.

However, Mao *was* tyrannical in the sense that he was, much to the chagrin of those closest to him, what one might call an 'annoying control freak'. 'Annoying control freaks' are humans whose 'chill buttons' are temporarily on the 'fritz' (or, in some extreme cases, permanently broken). Due to these faulty 'chill buttons', 'annoying control freaks' often feel it within their rights to influence, or preferably to assume totally uncontested control over any and all situations that may or may not have any impact whatsoever on their lives in the present, or in any conceivable future. 'Annoying control freaks' are usually at their worst when meeting new people, as they feel themselves incapable of 'going with the flow', or 'taking a chill pill', and thus often make poor first impressions when, say, meeting a new girlfriend's friends for the first time. This, of course, is a purely hypothetical example.

Anyhow, Mao was a writer. The guy had already penned (that means typed on a laptop) two modestly successful (that means not very successful at all) novels. However, in spite of the fact that he had a fairly clear idea of the subject matter he wished to explore in his next purely hypothetical novel, and in spite of the fact that he had done several months of research exploring this subject matter, some inexplicable blockage was preventing him from 'penning' the third novel, which would catapult him into Justin Bieber-like overnight success.

But the sad truth, dear reader, is that when you're after overnight success, there will always be the naysayers.

"Why don't you take a break, man?"

Some of his 'friends' suggested.

"You're, like, obsessed, dude."

They derp-derped.

Nevertheless, somewhat like very good tennis player and Zen master Novak Djokovic, who, at the prestigious 2019 Wimbledon Lawn Tennis Championships was able to mentally translate the crowd's rooting cries for archrival and all-around exquisite human being Roger Federer into what he heard as rooting cries for 'Novak Djokovic', Mao, too, had the ability to transambibulate reality into whatever he wanted it to be.

Wow, that was a wordy way to say that Mao is delusional and that we like tennis.

... and making up words.

Forgive us.

"Two novels before thirty is an unbelievable achievement! You are an unparalleled inspiration!"

He heard them yelp from the rooftops of his deranged mind.

Yes, clearly our beloved hero was a diligent, ambitious, and neurotic young man. He would have time to rest when he died, he thought, and even then, just think of the feats he could accomplish in the afterlife, freed from the constraints of space and time!

Now, this is no original insight, but this kind of overthinking and obsessive single-mindedness can really be bad for one's health. What's worse, it can really get in the way of having a good time. And alas, our dear hero Mao was, in fact, firmly knotted in the humdrum of what one might call an emotionally constipated existence.

Simply put: Mao was in a rut.

Allow us to explain.

For a time, Mao had felt that he had his petty little life absolutely figured out. For the last few months, he had finally landed and held onto a decent job. For the first time in his life, he was living without Mommy or Daddy in the next room. His writing career was steadily, if excruciatingly slowly, burgeoning. And, of course, he had found the love of his life.

Or, so he thought.

In spite of the perceived stability of his semi-charmed life (or, just perhaps due to it), Mao couldn't come up with a single damned thing to write.

Nada.

Zilch.

It had been that way for months.

He had this grand, overarching idea for his next novel: to write a serious and moving book about the 'post-generation', the 'postmodern condition', and the ways in which Western culture seemed to be over-analyzing and exploiting the idea of the 'I', almost to the point of its schizophrenic rupture, or worse, its paranoiac implosion.

Again, we suspect what you may be thinking. Do not worry, this won't be a Douglas Coupland homage. We aren't going to be sarcastically and self-indulgently exploring the ethos of an entire generation. Although, there will be sarcasm. And there will be tonnes of self-indulgence (if you hadn't yet noticed). There will be observations about the 'post-generation', too. But that won't be *all* there is. There will be other things. Plenty of other things.

In spite of Mao's grand idea, he could not seem to find a grand narrative in which to house his thoughts. He could not work out a way to bring his notions to fruition. His ideas seemed trapped in a vortex of abstraction, and though he had nurtured them in their embryonic forms for months, he had not yet birthed anything. This was torturous to him, as he waddled about, heavy with ideas refusing to kick, or to show any signs of life. And consequently, he was unable to feel passionately about any of them. However, something was clearly missing. He hadn't found the lightning in a bottle, the magic elixir that would bring it all together, the grease to put the wheels in motion, the... the... you get the idea. The man was simply uninspired. He had written two novels already, and they were doing okay in the sales department. He was glad to be making some money (it was his understanding that in the grand scheme of things, most artists do not). Yet, he was far, far from realizing his vivid dreams of concubines, servants, and palazzo paid for by paperback royalties.

Mao's other career, anyway, was going okay. That is to say, Mao worked at a very profitable 'not-for-profit' school, where he taught recently immigrated Chinese students to speak English gooder. He didn't love the job (it was an underutilization of his staggering genius, clearly), but it paid the bills, and the bills were bigger than ever before. Mao's favorite student at the school was a boy named Boning. He was a good-natured, semi-mute doofus sixteen years of age who really lifted Mao's spirits. Mao thought it was funny to think that with Boning's goofy personality, his socially awkward reluctance to express himself, and his just barely acceptable personal hygiene standards, that it would likely be a long while before Boning would find himself, well, you see where we're going with this...

Mao's students were nice, and he did help them, but deep down, he knew that helping people was simply not something that interested him very much.

Aside from his job... Oh! Yes. His apartment.

Mao's apartment was a large four-and-a-half in the Park-Extension borough of Montréal, Québec, Canada. Allow us to explain.

Canada is a large, cold, more than half-empty, some would say inconsequential country just north of the United States of America, whose national mythology is rooted in hockey, maple syrup, asking nicely, fossil fuel deposits, English-French language controversies, perpetual strife with First Nations peoples, apology and guilt, an ambivalence toward and even reluctance to define itself, and copious amounts of imported culture from its bolder and more decisive neighbor to the south. It is also one of the freest countries in the world and an overall lovely place to live, if you can hack it through the winter and all the red tape.

Québec is the only officially French province in Canada, and holds the prestige of instigating some (all) of the aforementioned English-French controversy. Although, it is also widely regarded for its distinctly Québécois cultural heritage, its *joie-de-vivre*, and its downright courageous tolerance of superfluous bureaucracy, incompetence and flippantly overt corruption.

Montréal is Québec's largest city, a multicultural agglomeration with a sizeable Anglophone minority that for whatever reason just refuses to lie down and die. It is also renowned as the pothole and orange traffic cone capital of the world. Overall, it's a fun city and a great cultural and culinary hub, though not as much if you don't speak French with the preferred rural twang... i.e. 'phock yew henglish cawliss'.

And finally, Park-Extension is a central, traditionally Greek, and now heavily Indo-Greek borough that has been Montréal's 'up-and-coming' darling for the last forty years. When Mao moved in, it was still coming.

Mao hadn't initially expected to find himself living in Park Extension. He came, in fact, from reasonably middle-class upbringing. In spite of this, though, the man himself was broke as a joke. He justified this in part by proclaiming himself a bohemian, or some other such flavor-of-the-month hippie shite. As he rationalized it, his financially imprudent move out of his rent-free parental lodgings into his apartment in Park-Extension would help him realize his romanticized notions of writing among the disenfranchised proles of his hometown. Unfortunately, most of that romance wore off just under two hours into his residency, when he realized that no amount of scrubbing was going to get rid of the grime caked into his bathroom tiles.

Mostly, though, the guy was twenty-seven years old! This is an age defined by an overwhelming desire for space, and to be left alone! All these reasons (rationalizations) converged as his hand danced across the lease, leaving his scribbly signature (and nearly all of his liquidity for the foreseeable future) behind.

The apartment was very large. That, Mao thought, was its greatest virtue. It was larger than any other apartment he would have been able to afford elsewhere, like the posh neighboring Mile End. The fact that it was a four-and-a-half meant that the apartment had a spare room, which really provided the wow-factor that convinced Mao this was the place. The sad reality, however, was that he seldom entered that spare room, where his library was neatly organized in alphabetical order on cheap Swedish shelves, his work desk was in a state of disuse and disarray, and miscellaneous belongings were scattered about haphazardly. There were also the two lingering bags of his ex-lover's things.

But we'll get to that.

The place was his, and he loved it for that reason. No longer was he forced to live in his father's cold, damp basement, where he would be regularly interrupted during very intimate moments with lover or left hand by his father's clumsy footsteps on the carpeted staircase, or, once, in the midst of a particularly enjoyable romp – he and she had found an old, obscure disco record whose strangely syncopated beats produced new and unexpected movements, and so, new and unexpected delights – by his father's somewhat tightly coiled inamorata, walking down to the cold room to fetch some onions, but stumbling, instead, upon something more fragrant on the way, and that also brought tears to everyone's eyes.

Events like that one had expedited Mao's exit, despite how financially imprudent it was for him to be renting. Still, the palazzo called, and the apartment was to be the first stepping-stone.

Please forgive all the circuitous explanations. It's just that the year 2019 A.D. on planet Earth of the Milky Way galaxy was a complicated time. We are a complicated organism. Things are not going to be simple.

When are they ever?

You see, sweet reader, living in one's parent's basement well into one's twenties was an epiphenomenon extremely common with the slowly blossoming youth of Generation Y (also interchangeably referred to as the Millennials, Generation Why?, or the Post-Generation). This was partly because legions of fresh-faced dupes possessing expensive, but deceptively worthless arts and humanities degrees ventured out into the desert wasteland of the North American job market every year, to compete fruitlessly with legions of other dupes with identical qualifications and worldviews, only to settle for jobs slightly-to-completely unrelated to their fields of 'expertise', unless they were of the dull few passionate about bookkeeping or digital media consulting, where they would earn yearly salaries of approximate equal value to the yearly tuition costs that got them into this sad predicament to begin with.

Perhaps that is a little exaggerated, but it isn't nearly as exaggerated as you'd hope.

Anyhow, we think that pretty well sums up what you need to know about Mao. Well, everything except the girl. But then, the girl probably deserves her own feature, right?

II

Before her, Mao had never really been in love. He had never looked at life through the fabled rose-colored lens, seen a woman on the other side, and then *actually* gotten to be with her. He had girlfriends, sure. He told them he loved them, sure. But did he? Maybe. But he didn't the way he did this girl. Or, perhaps that is simply, what do you call that? Recency bias? The concept that explains why things that happened more recently seem more important than things that happened a long time ago, and which also might explain why human beings remain so ignorant to history that it becomes doomed to repeat itself...?

Anyway, we're fairly sure it wasn't that.

Mao loved her.

He really, really did!

The girl...

Hm, this anonymity won't do. We'll have to ascribe her a name.

Ah, yes!

We'll call her A–Z, because in Mao's alphabet, she was the first, the last, and every letter in between. It's a fitting pseudonym, we think, as Mao's idealization of her femininity is one of the things that ultimately led to his inability to view her soberly as the flawed individual she was, consequently playing a big role in undermining the communication pathways in their relationship, which caused a toxic codependent behavioral pattern to develop, thus ensuring the relationship's inevitable demise.

Or, at least, this was one of Mao's longwinded retrospectives.

Mao loved A–Z in a way he hadn't loved other girls before. She was his best friend. She got his sense of humor and he got hers. They had similar tastes in music. Their physical chemistry was off the charts.

He loved her in a way that made him feel okay sacrificing the potential of countless other mates for her, and her alone for all of eternity. You'll have to excuse the evocative language, it's only that 'potential other mates' are a strong impulse for a growing boy. He thought he felt this way, anyway. But then, as time passed and the two of them slowly settled into a routine, Mao began to feel the creeping urge that had caused him to flee his previous relationships: a growing desire to break free from the warm, fuzzy, predictably padded room where the excitement had begun to stale.

He began to think more often about rock stars, whom he naturally admired. He thought about the way these rock stars lived – fornicating 'til they got their fill, doing a bunch of drugs, and seemingly having things their way at all times. Going about this gloomy way, Mao began to hate the comfort and stability of his love life with A–Z, and slowly but surely sabotaged it.

When A-Z cooked for Mao, it was too salty. When A-Z did something nice for Mao, he sought the ulterior motive. When A-Z did pretty much anything, Mao felt he could have done it better himself. *Bref,* when A-Z made any sort of suggestion, or took any sort of action whatsoever, Mao found the flaw in it, and refused to see anything but that flaw.

Eventually, A-Z lost interest in this setup. She was a self-respecting gal, and Mao simply wasn't the man she had fallen in love with anymore. So, in spite of the difficulty and the pain, she ended things.

Mao had mixed feelings about the split. For one, it hurt. He was sure he had meant it when he called this woman the love of his life, and yet she had walked away from him without so much as a glance over the shoulder. It was difficult for him to understand.

On the other hand, there was an undeniable part of him that felt excited.

We know that sounds a little insane.

You see, reader, in the dying months of their relationship, Mao gradually began, in his melancholy way, to fall prey to that most pernicious of all clichés.

Mao, with all of his bohemian proclivities, began to fixate on the idea that a *true artist* must *suffer* to create *great art.*

A-Z had been in his way the entire time! It was no wonder he could not write. He was far too happy. He had been overly satisfied! He had been excessively sated! And ultimately, this had caused him to become sedate! His perceived happiness with A–Z, blocking his creative outlet, his writing, his *raison d'être,* began to make him unhappy. Ensnared in this perfectly logical paradox, Mao drove himself subconsciously to unhappiness and suffering, which would, he subconsciously presumed, inspire him to write, and so in turn, finally make him happy! However, the thing was, now that he was rid of the pesky 'love of his life', Mao wasn't feeling any more expressive. Neither, dear reader, was he feeling any more inspired. Since the split, Mao felt more, sure, but he always seemed to be feeling more of the same thing:

Regret.

This turn of events made absolutely no sense to him, and undermined the stability of his carefully-constructed worldview.

He thought often of those rock stars, and his literary mind couldn't help but make the connection between their self-destruction through drugs and polygamy, and the mythical hero's journey into the underworld. There was danger, certainly, and great risk, but profound truths were learned upon that journey, and encountering these profound truths head on was precisely what confirmed the hero's, or rock star's status. Risking it all to return from the land of the dead with something beautiful and helpful in the land of the living: that was the hero's destiny! Like Nikki Sixx returning from heroin overdose to grace the land of the living with 'Kickstart My Heart'. It was a tale as old as time!

But then, why wasn't it working for him? Why couldn't he, in spite of the suffering, write? The impediment was gone... Perhaps it was that he wasn't suffering *enough*? Perhaps a cocaine, or crystal meth dependency would expedite his creative reawakening?

It was certainly food for thought.

All Mao knew was that he felt terrible, like he had one foot in the underworld and the other in a big pile of dog doo-doo.

According to conventional wisdom, the thing to do was to wait.

And so, he did.

Time and distance usually offer perspective.

It was only a matter of time.

His masterpiece would undoubtedly rise up from out of the ruins.

III

Alright, so you've been introduced to Mao, and to his conundrum.

Introducing the main character is always pretty high up on the storyteller's checklist, so it's good that we got that out of the way. However, as we're sure you already know, stories with just one character aren't usually very interesting.

When's the last time you spent your precious time watching a one man show? Never, right. Even the greatest characters of all time like Jesus H. Christ, the Batman and Ash Ketchum of Pallet Town would be absolutely worthless without their massive supporting casts.

Certainly, evolved from this primordial soup of influences, Mao could be no different.

Mao's supporting cast... well, actually, that sounds too trivial. Mao's destiny? Yes, that's better. Mao's *destiny* was, as is so often the case, hidden in plain sight, invisible to fate's pawn while at a mere arm's length. His destiny had taken human form, and it was coming for him, straight on. There was nothing he could do to escape it.

But, we'll get to that.

While Mao was dealing with the inner turmoil of his stupidity-induced sadness, Mr. Jajùmissu Cá, on the other hand, was rebuilding his life entirely from the ground up. You see, just and gentle reader, Mr. Cá had just arrived in Cá-nada. He had had to travel, however, a fairly hard road to get there. It wasn't easy immigrating to another country, especially one where you didn't speak either of the two languages so well, and where not a single person in the new country knew a single thing, or had a single care about your homeland. Jajùmissu Cá, well, the poor guy had it rough! Luckily, although Jajùmissu Cá (we'll refer to him interchangeably as J.C. from now on, just to make things easier for all of us) had left his home country in a hurry, he had carried along with him a fairly sizeable nest egg. This, at least, was a silver lining. J.C. used to have a good job back home. A very good job. But in Canada, he had run into a problem.

Back in his home country of Mimijad, Jajùmissu Cá had been raised by a stern military man. His father, the Lieutenant Vàtene Dà Cá, believed very firmly in the twenty-first century dictum that specialization was the readiest path to success. J.C., hardly having a choice in the matter, followed his wise, disciplinary father's advice to heed the dictum, and did so with unwavering dedication. Under his father's watchful eye, J.C. studied very, very hard in grade school. His work ethic impressed all of his teachers, and then later, all of his professors at the Univerzzidad dé Mimijad. However, J.C. was not just book smart. He was also cunning enough to make the most of the networking potential of a University experience (i.e. shamelessly pandering to the campus elites). It wasn't very long before J.C. became a regular in all the 'right circles'. J.C. built his reputation as a rigorous intellectual through his graduate work, which was precisely as tedious and obscure as it needed to be, to tickle his academic supervisor's tedious and obscure Mimijadian whiskers. Everyone agreed his citations showed great promise. And after five short years, and the completion of an eighty-page thesis that no less than four people absentmindedly skimmed through, J.C. finally accepted his doctorate, and in so doing, realized his lifelong dream of becoming the first ever certified, accredited, and internationally-recognized Mimijadian Meerkat Behavioral Expert (M.M.B.E.). With this unbelievably specialized (and so very unlikely to be automated) expertise in tow, Jajùmissu Cá secured a job at the Mimijad Zoo straight out of school (the lucky bastard). There, he started off as an animal keeper – a job which offered him the pleasure of developing an excellent rapport with the animals, and especially, of course, with his beloved Mimijadian meerkats. As a consequence of that opportunity, and after only three short years of networking, leveraging, and finessing, J.C finally managed to supplant the incumbent Director, who, it must be stated, was a rather horribly outdated boomer who struggled with Microsoft Excel, and who was merely coasting on his seniority and old school 'people skills'. This, dear reader, was how J.C. managed to ascend to the highly prestigious position of Director of the Mimijad Zoo.

Alright, let's take a breather.

We suppose there are a few things we should clarify.

Firstly, Mimijad is a small, extremely remote island nation located in the Mozambique Channel, with a population of just under a quarter of a million. It's renowned for its sprawling beaches and biodiversity. If you've never heard of it, it's probably because of the egotism and inherent bias of Eurocentric Western educational systems, which trivialize non-Imperial cultures as primitive, or unenlightened. We suppose it is not absolutely necessary, but it would be appropriate here for you to take a moment to revel in self-disgust for your privilege.

Secondly, we have absolutely nothing against boomers. We just think it is high time they all retire, so as to give the basement-dwelling millennials a chance to ascend to lives above ground.

And thirdly, Mimijadian meerkats are very similar to regular meerkats, except that their fur is a light shade of purple. This is due, experts assert, to their diet having evolved to consist mostly of Mimijad's most abundant crop, which is beetroot.

Unfortunately, Jajùmissu Cá's triumph at the Mimijad Zoo was destined to be short-lived. It was only a few years later, just as J.C.'s career as Zoo Director was really starting to take off, that Mimijad succumbed to a major political upheaval. A bloody civil war was waged between the ruthless Mimijadian Republicans and the frantic Free State of Mimijad Coalition. It was the bloodiest, cruelest war in Mimijad's long and illustrious history. Tensions had always existed between the two scarcely distinguishable factions, but to explain the minutiae would simply be beyond the scope of our historical knowledge. However, if you were interested, we would direct you to B.F. Jabālitsa's incredibly thorough *The History of the Great Nation of Mimijad* available through Univerzzidad dé Mimijad Press. Although, it may be hard for a North American to get his or her or they or them's hands on a copy, as *The History of the Great Nation of Mimijad* is one of the few consumer goods not yet available for one click purchase or same day delivery. Anyhow, these aforementioned tensions rose to a fever pitch, and sparked the murderous war. The Mimijadian Civil War was not unusual in that it was motivated by economics. However, it does hold the distinction of being the only war in the history of humankind to be waged over the control of a nation's lucrative beetroot exports.

The majority of the Mimijadian populace committed themselves fully to the Great War, which turned families against one another in bloody combat. As an intellectual and a pacifist with no very strong political affiliations, J.C. quickly realized he must flee Mimijad. This would be no easy task, as the Mimijadian Republicans had seized control of the country's seaports, while the Free State of Mimijad Coalition now controlled Mimijad's only airport. Travel to and from Mimijad had become heavily restricted. What's more, J.C. was a good and proud Mimijadian.

The idea of permanently leaving his motherland was something that took a large psychological toll on him. However, in spite of the challenges he faced, the man persevered.

It took nearly all of his cunning, but J.C. forged a plan.

As the Zoo Director, Jajùmissu Cá was something of a celebrity in Mimijad, and so was privy to certain... privileges. He had friends in high places, and he had plenty of Mimijadian currency (though unfortunately, J.C would soon learn that the buying power of one Mimijadian mimeck was the equivalent of about 0.00004 Canadian dollars – a fact that would later cause our poor Jajùmissu Cá to fall to his knees and weep like a child, while holding up the line at the currency exchange desk, and forcing the apathetic and overweight employee behind the counter to sigh and call security). J.C. knew how to grease the right mimeck-hungry palms. He cited the urgent need for a Mimijadian representative at a prestigious international zoo convention in New York City. As Zoo Director, it only made sense that he would have to go. At great personal expense, J.C. was finally cleared to board one of the extremely rare flights out of Mimijad, with only a few other high-profile Mimijadians.

Naturally, shrewd and intelligent reader, the zoo convention was all pretense. You see, there was no zoo convention in New York City. We mean, there might have been. There are yearly pee fetish conventions in that crazy depraved town, so in all likelihood there *was* also a zoo convention. However, the simple question the

Mimijadian officials had neglected to ask while greedily counting their mimecks was this: even if there *was* a zoo convention in New York City, why would a Mimijadian representative *urgently* need to attend? Didn't it occur to anyone that this was the first time that a Mimijadian Zoo Director had ever even suggested attending a zoo convention outside of the country? First of all, Mimijad is a tiny island nation with only one zoo, and it is mostly occupied by purple meerkats. Secondly, putting that aside, why would *any* zoo convention *urgently* need to be attended? It's a completely ludicrous excuse for needing to leave the country in the midst of a bloody civil war. It's so ludicrous that it almost casts doubt on J.C. and his entire backstory. But then, maybe we're reading too much into it. The insane things mortals are willing to believe never cease to astonish us.

Very, very few made it out of Mimijad in those dark times. It is estimated that at least one third of the Mimijadian population was wiped out in the ten years that spanned the Mimijadian Civil War.

Luckily, J.C. was a relatively young man who had no wife or children (and, secretly, no desire for either... but not because he was gay, though that would be totally okay, in 2019 in most places in the West, though not in 2019 in Mimijad, but that's also okay, because it's a different culture, or maybe it isn't okay, because everyone should have the right to express themselves... eh, we should have left this one alone). J.C. was mentally strong, and he knew that he needed to restart (it's just that he actually wasn't gay, so we just thought it would be a relevant detail moving forward). He came to terms with his fate remarkably quickly, and managed to keep himself together (look, we're completely for two, three, or even five grown men sucking each other off in a steamy, overcrowded, and questionably sanitized bathhouse under the loving, watchful eyes of their god, and we will not stand for anyone telling you a single thing that in any way suggests otherwise!). He left his heritage, his parents, his meerkats, and his legacy behind when he boarded that flight. He embarked on a journey to chase the Canadian Dream (the same as the American Dream, just colder, with higher taxes and more apologizing), and from that moment on there was no turning back. Just hours after landing, Jajùmissu Cá took the first train out of New York, and erased once and for all any trace of his past life.

Remarkably, the Mimijadian seemed unfazed by either the cold, or the inquisitive glances at his caramel skin and exotic Mimijadian garments. He was a smart man. He had done some research. It was all to be expected. For all he knew, he might be the only Mimijadian in all of Canada!

To clarify, J.C's wherewithal (still reasonable despite the exchange rate) enabled him to employ certain specialized agencies, which greatly expedited the process of cutting through all the red tape of visas, permanent residency, and so on. However, one thing his oodles of charm and bags of money couldn't help with was the fact that he did not speak a lick of French. In fact, Jajùmissu Cá's pronunciation of 'Bonjour' was so agonizingly brutal that you could almost hear the ghosts of René Lévesque and Jacques Parizeau screaming for another referendum in the infinitely echoing halls of the afterlife. As such, J.C. found himself desperately bereft of gainful employment in the meerkat-free and bureaucratically mangled wilderness of Montréal. He could survive for a little while on his dwindling mimecks, fine, but how long could he survive without the sense of purpose he derived from righteously occupying a position of expertise, or without the loving babble of his meerkats? J.C. needed something more than money. He needed that most elusive of all things: self-actualization!

Considering his pitiful employment opportunities, and after a lot of careful reflection that concluded with definitely ruling out prostitution, J.C. felt that he was left with one choice, and one choice only: total and utter rebrand.

Once settled in the Park Extension apartment he had managed to secure through a series of hesitant and awkward phone calls on the train to Montréal, Jajùmissu Cá spent his first few weeks in Cá-nada watching dozens upon dozens of hours of internet videos. You know, to acclimate himself to the culture. Then, the crafty rascal scoured both Pinterest and the blogosphere desperately seeking inspo, until finally, he had his *eureka!* moment: he would put his entrepreneurial skills and oodles of charm to work by creating a YouTube channel about divining! Now *this* piqued his interest! *This* was something that would provide the new and engaging challenge he was looking for! The existing channels about fortune telling, occultism, and energy cleansing already garnered millions upon millions of views, and there were countless resources at his disposal to help him penetrate the market!

J.C. rolled up his sleeves and got to work. He watched YouTube video upon YouTube video about everything from crystal balls to palm readings, and most importantly, tarot cards. In a mere three weeks, J.C. was able to complete an online course certifying him as a Certified Tarot Reader (C.T.R.). Ingeniously leveraging his exotic mien, the inspiration he derived from social media mood boards and that one marketing elective he had taken at the Univerzzidad dé Mimijad, J.C. began to slowly but surely shroud himself in *bona fide* supernatural airs.

As our clever, and no doubt attractive reader is certainly aware, no veritable rebrand would be complete without a clever name. And so, the *Mystic of Mimijad* was born.

To clarify once more, a 'mystic' is a person who tries their best to convince you that things that aren't real, are actually the most real, and that things that are real, actually aren't all that real. Paraphrasing Google's definition, a 'mystic' is a person who seeks by contemplation and self-surrender to obtain unity with or absorption into the Deity or the absolute, or who believes in the spiritual apprehension of truths that are beyond the intellect. Okay, so we didn't paraphrase that at all. But Google is basically expressing the same thing we did in wordier words.

In all seriousness though, about this New Age/ Mysticism/ Spiritualism stuff: it isn't that the crystals or the cards have any inherent magic to them, or any ability to solve any actual problems. It is more that they represent things, or concepts, or feelings, and that these things or concepts or feelings they represent are fluid, and malleable, and so both infinitely relatable, and infinitely interpretable. It is through the interpretation of these symbols, or ideas, or metaphors, which are attached to deeply ingrained feelings or modes of thought, that one is able to unlock the hidden cache deep within themselves, and come to emotional or psychological epiphany, thus transcending (hopefully) the problem they initially turned to mysticism to solve.

Right. Those were even wordier words than Google used.

It was said that back in his home country, the mystic was renowned for the calm he exuded, and, of course, for the unspeakable profundity of his mystic abilities. So much was the timeless man revered, and so immersed was he in his spiritual awakening and union with the divine godhead, that he had achieved the ultimate self-mortification and so entirely shed his personal, individualized identity. It was for this reason that he preferred that all would refer to him by the impersonal moniker The Mystic of Mimijad. Journeyers from all walks of life would make the pilgrimage to the rolling hills of Mimijad for a word with the illustrious one. However, so spiritually pure was he, that he felt it his duty to uproot himself, abdicating the comforts of national fame that had dulled his passion for truth, and instead offering himself up to the wanting and spiritually bankrupt masses of Montréal. As part of his great sacrifice, he settled for a mangy, sparsely furnished three-and-a-half in Park-Ex, where he would break his fast only when absolutely necessary, and more often than not with his preferred boiled beetroot and boxed macaroni and cheese dinner.

Jajùmissu Cá, only forty years old, dyed his short but thick black hair snow white, so as to look older, and consequently, wiser. He donned long, flowing, vaguely spiritual Mimijadian robes and passed around shiny flyers and business cards out on the street. He slipped these into mailboxes, posted them onto public announcement boards, and wedged them under windshield wipers.

Unsurprisingly, it was only a matter of days before the calls started flooding in, and J.C. was ready for them. He had been brushing up on his sales techniques.

Reader, YouTube really is a marvelous resource. In 2019, there wasn't anything in the world one couldn't do with just a little bit of elbow grease, and a whole lot of YouTube.

When an Indian man called, J.C. affected his best Indian accent, and spoke vaguely of the same-not-sameness of the Atman and Brahman, while suggesting that the man come see him for a free consultation. When a Mediterranean-sounding accent echoed through the phone, he told them the root of their troubles was that someone had no doubt cursed them with the *malocchio,* or the evil eye, that he could certainly cast it away, and to come see him about a free consultation. When a lonely white woman called (and these really were the vast majority of the calls), he told them in a gruff, sultry voice that he could divine the root of their unhappiness and sexual frustration through a combination of palm and tarot readings, but only if they came to see him for a free consultation.

And so, the Mystic of Mimijad's legend slowly grew, and Montréal began to take notice. People from every borough began to turn to him for his divine experience, his access to the world beyond appearances, his deeper understanding of the universal truth, and most importantly, for his ability to expedite his clients' personal transformation. The proof, after all, was always in the pudding.

J.C., likewise, was absolutely thrilled with the success of his rebrand, and with his new life as an independent contractor.

IV

Reader, you may be wondering at this stage in the proceedings just who we are, and whether you should trust us. If you weren't wondering that, then you can probably just skip this section and continue on to the next feature. But, we mean, how could you not be wondering that? What kind of mindless meat puppet are you?

Anyway, our identity is of little import.

Don't worry about it.

We choose to identify as non-identifiable.

Our preferred pronouns are 'nunya' and 'bizniss'.

You may think of us simply as your nameless, faceless, incorporeal narrator. We're like your guardian angel, always watching over you. In a harmless, benevolent kind of way! Though you might want to get that rash checked out. Yes, we are always watching over you, in a benevolent, guiding, only occasionally mocking kind of way. In that way, we're also kind of like fate. Oh, we like that, actually. That tickles us just so. Yes. That makes the most sense. You should think of us like fate. If you want to. Otherwise, do only what feels right to you.

If it would make you more comfortable to put a more 'personal' spin on things, or to think of us as an individualized entity that has an individualized personality, then let us offer a wonderfully fun fact about us: we are completely enamored with the Arctic Monkeys' 2018 album *Tranquility Base Hotel &* *Casino*, which polarized listeners with its brazen departure from the Monkeys' previously guitar-driven rock sounds, favoring a more loungy, science-fiction-inspired retro-futuristic vibe, and a prominent jazz piano presence.

We were kind of lukewarm about it when it was initially released. We mean, we didn't really understand it, but we came around to it in a big way, and now we think that it is without a doubt among their finest work.

We mean, we really think that front man and songwriter Alex Turner hit so many nails right on the head when it comes to <u>twenty-first century satire</u>. The album really throws so many elements of modern, ahem, <u>postmodern</u> life into your face as you're listening. We mean, to name a few: <u>target marketing</u>, <u>globalization</u>, <u>consumerism</u>, <u>escapism</u>, <u>vice</u>, <u>the allure of instant gratification</u>, <u>the universal pursuit of fame</u>, <u>review culture</u>, <u>social credit</u>, <u>post-truth</u>, <u>automation</u>, <u>technological dependence</u>, <u>data collection</u>, and <u>the apathy twenty-first century humans feel towards what was once nothing but a dystopian nightmare and is now everyday reality</u>.

Even the title, *Tranquility Base Hotel & Casino* is in and of itself a paradox and oxymoron that nods impishly at the notion of our <u>modern day commodification of everything</u>, including the most fundamental and once inviolably sacred-eternal tenets that formerly upheld our churches, temples and all types of places of worship, and now, instead, hold up billboards for fragrances, streaming services, or home equity lines of credit. And of course, there's the oh-so-salient and repeated comparison of smartphones to everything from portals, black holes, and mirror-mirror-on-the-wall's.

Hosanna! Hosanna! They've fallen from grace...

The album is great. It's just, great.

Some people called the album self-indulgent. It is, but we think in a sexy, self-aware kind of way. It's not for everyone, though, and that's okay. We even heard one guy say:

"*Tranquility Base Hotel & Casino* sounds like Alex Turner fellating himself... in space."

We mean, gee, that guy went a little overboard. He was probably just jealous. The album is self-indulgent, but what isn't these days?

Before that album, we liked the Arctic Monkeys, but, you know, we liked them. We didn't like *AM* nearly as much as their other stuff, thought it was a bit of a sellout job, undeniably appealing to the womenfolk nonetheless, over a billion plays on streaming services and all, and we could listen to it without shuddering or anything like that. Before *Tranquility Base Hotel & Casino*, we thought they were a rock band with a sexy bent and a British accent that had a bit of a sentimentality and nostalgia about them. We mean, we liked them. But after *Tranquility Base Hotel & Casino*, oh, ho, ho, ho, we love them! Bloody brilliant.

Gobsmacked. Spot on, mate. Sporting. Fifty quid. Bloody limeys, innit?

Well, we think that's about all there is to tell about us...

Overall, we're rooting for Mao, but at the same time we've a feeling that the whole thing may well just, end up too clever, for its own good, ta nanananananananana na, the way some science fiction does.

We did not get permission to use that line, but good luck suing us Mr. Turner. We're incorporeal, remember? Maybe you can serve us up the papers over some tacos at the Information Action Ratio. But then, we just wanted to be one of those ghosts, you thought that, you could sue...

V

A few weeks into his separation from A-Z, Mao was still feeling bummed. However, it was Halloween, and so, he put a wig on and donned some black eyeliner (although, reader, Mao never, not even for a second thought about putting any more than that single accentuating line of black on his face, as he had absolutely no aspirations of becoming the Prime Minister of Canada) and went to a party. If you are wondering what kind of party it was, rest assured it was both as scandalous and depraved as any you have been to. Suffice to say, it was a party abounding with stupidity. Except, everyone was getting a little older this time around. And so, the intoxicants were consumed a little earlier, perhaps in only very slightly smaller quantities, and perhaps with only very slightly less gusto than in previous years. Repetition dulls even the sharpest knife, as they say.

Maybe that was only Mao's troubled perception, though.

In an attempt to escape his troubles, Mao got so disastrously inebriated that he lost his wig, and his regret over the whole affair was only redoubled with the onset of a remarkably powerful headache the next day. However, there was a silver lining to all this nonsense. Mao realized something in the morning, as he rolled over to take a look at his trusty black mirror.

He had written something the night before, in his notes!

The Cliché

Euphoria! And then, yes! It was coming back! He remembered making his way to the washroom, very urgently, to get away from the distractions and to capture this first lucid flash of inspiration in what seemed ages!

Here is what our inebriated hero wrote (remember, the first thing he had written in months!) in the 'Notes' application of his black mirror:

Excerpt from Mao's Notes
31/10/2019
HALLOWEEN, CANDY

Candy makes you sick, right?

So, Nestle, Mars, Hershey, and all the other big, and not so big (looking at you Tootsie) Halloween players are pushing a nefarious agenda, perpetuating the Evil Empire's Chocolate-Industrial-Complex and even bringing Big Pharma into the racket.

'What kind of half-baked conspiracy is this?' you might ask.

Well, you just shut your chocolate goop-filled mouth and I'll tell you how it is!

Consider this: Halloween comes right before the winter every single year. Candy binging weakens your immune system. The combination of weakened immune system and dropping temperatures is all but sure to make you sick. Sick people buy high-margin syrups and lozenges.

You do the math.

What percentage of Nestle's sales are generated in the two weeks insulating Halloween? It's an asinine pagan holiday celebrating monsters and ghouls, yet they market it so cleverly that it only feels natural to eat a bunch of artificially sweetened poison. What in the sweet sacrificial fuck does a chocolate-covered wafer have to do with the spirits of the underworld? Ghosts don't even eat. Does the irony of a miniature 'Mr. Big' protect against a poltergeist the way a clove of garlic protects against a vampire? That would be clever, and plausible enough, really, if they'd even bother to hire a few morally bankrupt writers to cook up a logical premise for the sugar binge. Instead, they don't, because they don't need a logical premise to convince our submissive, emulsified mush for brains to eat miniature chocolates every day for a month straight. All they need are bright lights, wide-spanning distribution, retail placement, and enough on-screen repetition. Yeah, too much candy will make you sick. And not just the kind made by Nestle, and not just at Halloween.

Reading this the next day, Mao was surprised. He wasn't sure what to be more surprised about: about how lucid the rant was, or about how irrelevant. But the note had jogged his memory. He recalled typing it up on his handheld device while urinating, on shaky knees, somehow miraculously keeping it all free of spelling mistakes, and even more miraculously, keeping it all in the bowl.

He recalled, too, as he was leaving the washroom, noticing that just a single drop of his urine had splashed onto the toilet seat, which he had forgotten to put up, and which made the unlikely feat of keeping it all in the bowl at least three times as impressive. He recalled very vividly how he stared long and hard at that one drop of urine on the toilet seat, contemplating its meaning. How did that one drop, among the countless sprayed into the toilet, manage to make its way out? How many drops, he wondered, of someone else's piss were needed to inspire disgust? Was it one? Two? Three? Did it matter if it was a stranger's, or an intimate's?

And then, he thought about A–Z.

Mao stayed in bed all of the rest of that day, his pounding headache thumping to the syncopated beat of his broken heart.

VI

There's something about hangovers, it would seem, that always brings the best out of a writer. Maybe it's the way that the suffering of excesses recently passed forces one's full immersion into the present reality, compelling the individual to painfully submit that everything outside of the present reality, in this case a reality of suffering, is entirely irrelevant. And then, if only that thought were as easy to hold onto in joy as it is in despair. Perhaps that is why hangovers offer access to that secret reserve of detachment and objectivity – a reserve normally inaccessible to the sober, hinderingly pluralistic mind. Maybe we're reading too much into it. Maybe Mao simply gathered some momentum with his Halloween rant, and was able to write something else running on those whiskey fumes. Maybe he had finally lifted the veil, and seen the beautiful face of his loving, lifelong partner: inspiration.

Whatever did it, Mao managed to write this the night after Halloween:

Excerpt From Mao's Notes
1/11/2019
PATHETIC FALLACY

I listen to the Smiths so Morrissey can put me in a mood introspective and melancholy enough to write. But what a cliché he's selling: the world sucks and nothing is as it seems and we are all destined to be lonely until we perish so what's the point of it all? That's all true, I guess, but focusing on it is such a drag. So, what, then? Willful delusion? We all live in some sort of willful delusion, so why should I consider myself the martyr who needs to point out the inherent hypocrisy of man? Well, I suppose, just because everyone is doing something doesn't mean it's right.

No matter how far you push your bounds they will never encapsulate everything. This is the curse of finitude. And everything you know and feel and experience is just the little bubble that encapsulates, and imprisons you. Or, at least, it is the bounds of what 'you' means to you. Your sense of self, I suppose.

Some people have larger bubbles than others, but none ever succeed in piercing through. This is an axiom of existence.

It is cold outside.

It is raining.

They call it pathetic fallacy when the main character of a story affects certain characteristics of his environment, or when nature acts out in accordance to a character's feelings.

I suppose this is 'pathetic' because in fiction, both character and environment are creations of the same maker. And so, the maker can easily fabricate the pathos to unite his creations. I suppose this is a 'fallacy' because in the real world, independent entities rarely empathize with one another, and there is no unifying maker.

Perhaps that last part is too cynical.

Perhaps it is misguided to think we don't feel a certain pathos or connection with our physical environment in the real world outside of books. Like character and setting, we must ultimately share the same maker as our environment, whether on any given day that maker prefers the title of Chance or Design.

We are not ashamed to say, reader, that that brought a tear to our eye. Well, we don't really have eyes, or tear ducts, because we don't really have a body, but we're trying to speak in metaphors you can understand here.

Maybe the kid has got what it takes...

Just because he has been writing in fits and starts, does not mean that the fragments are not valid, or connected, right? Not everything needs to have a clearly defined path, or narrative, does it? Maybe Mao will create his narrative retrospectively, making sense of his slapdash stew of feelings and ideas once the relief of distance offers its gift of perspective. Some moods are best experienced as passing. This is simply for the best. Wise men will know: concentrated melancholia is *meant* to be a passing mood. Much like an erection. Very much like an erection, if your melancholy lasts for more than six hours at a time, you're strongly urged to contact your nearest healthcare professional.

VII

And then, oh so suddenly, it was that saddest of months.

November.

With its cold, heartbreaking November rain.

Mao felt disillusioned.

It had been over two months since he had heard from A–Z.

He wondered what she was thinking. He wondered what she was feeling. He wondered if she missed him. He wondered what she was doing. He wondered *who* she was doing. It drove him up the walls.

When he was agitated, Mao often turned to the respite of a bottomless bowl of Rice Kirspeez (no trademark) cereal. This therapeutic ritual helped him snop, crockle, and pip (also no trademark) his way out of even the most concerning of conundrums.

However, on that particular cold, rainy November day in Park-Extension, Mao was out of milk.

And so, being a pragmatic and proactive guy, he decided to make a grocery run to get some.

Hurriedly plopping on a hat and coat, Mao scurried out of his top floor Apartment #7 into the yellowing walls of the building's common area and whizzed down the narrow stairwell. As he dashed by, Mao contemplated the meaning of the black and white checkered tiles below his feet, and decided that they made him feel eerie, like his life was taking place on a movie set. A Quentin Tarantino movie set, perhaps. His life was kooky enough to be a Tarantino film, wasn't it? The dialogue was certainly zany enough. The characters were certainly outrageous enough. But then, maybe it was missing some of the violence expected of a Tarantino. Maybe there was something he could do about that. There was violence in his novels, anyway. As he hit the middle floor, Mao wondered whether there was anything more relatable than a dingy stairwell. Maybe the stuffy office where everyone hates their job, and there's one guy who's just about to finally *do* something about it. That could potentially be violent...

His footsteps pattered down the stairs.

Mao reached the tiny lobby of his building, and was still muttering to himself when he noticed the strange man coming in through the out door. The very first thing Mao noticed about the man, aside from the eye-catching pink hue of his robes, was that in spite of the miserable cold and rain beyond the vestibule, the man was not wearing a raincoat. In fact, he was not wearing any coat at all. Instead, the man wore layers upon layers of flowing fuchsia robes that Mao couldn't quite place. Culturally, that is. He had never seen anything like them. Here was just this hulking frame of a man, his robes, and beneath them, yes, Mao was seeing that right, open-toed sandals on caramel feet. Outside, pouring rain.

On the giant's feet, sandals. Cold November rain. Pink robes. Bags of groceries.

Now, *this* Tarantino would love.

The man had five plastic grocery bags with him. Two were filled with miscellaneous items, one of them visibly outlined the macaroni and cheese boxes crammed within, and the other two were filled to the *brim* with what looked to Mao like... beetroot? That was odd. Who could possibly eat that much beetroot? And these bags were full, sweet and generous reader, full! As in not a *single* additional beetroot could have possibly been stuffed into the bag without seriously compromising its structural integrity. Macaroni and cheese. Beetroot. Fuchsia robes. Pouring rain. Sandals. The scene had it all.

However surreal it all seemed to Mao, the strange man was, in reality, fumbling about a cluttered key ring, looking for the one in a million that would grant him blessed access to the decrepit building, and soon thereafter relief from the great burden of all that beetroot.

Registering the fact that the man seemed to be confident of entering the building, and that the scene unfolding before him was simply too farfetched to be staged for some criminal purpose, Mao deduced he must be meeting the new tenant.

He thought it odd that he had never seen this man before. After all, Mao had been living in the building for a few months. And he was certain he would have remembered *this* character. He knew the apartment across from his was vacant when he moved in. Come to think of it, Mao had recently begun hearing sounds emanating from Apartment #8 across the hall. These sounds were... peculiar. Some, he had never heard before. There were sounds like chimes, incantations, and every now and then, guttural frequencies. Strange noises that, well, somehow seemed to fit together with the appearance of this strange man.

While Mao stood there putting it all together, the man kept on fiddling with his keys, struggling to find the right one with his hands full, and stubbornly refusing to put the bags down. He was leering at Mao, who was just standing there lost in reverie, as if to say: 'C'mon, brother, I know I'm foreign and maybe a little weird-looking, but help a guy out for goodness sake!' Mao, finally catching one of these glances and realizing he was being very rude, moved forward to open the door for the man and let him into the building.

"Oh, why, oh! Thank you my dear young man!"

'Dear young man?' Mao thought. 'And what in the world is that accent?'

The man towered over him, benevolently looking down at Mao, who was quite frankly overwhelmed by the newcomer's formidable size. For a brief moment, the two stared soundlessly at one another. Aside from his impressive stature, Mao was impressed by the profound, reassuring calm that seemed to emanate from deep within the strange man's face. The man, on the other hand, was concerned by the confusion and uncertainty that seemed to emanate from Mao's.

"No problem, sir. You must be my new neighbor. Apartment #8? Welcome to the building."

The man nodded, his eyes crinkling with delight.

"Oh, why, oh! Thank you so much? Yes! I am very honored to be here. Yes! Park-Extension is such a lovely neighborhood! Yes?"

Mao wondered if he was being ironic. Then he remembered the pink robes.

"Yes. I agree. It is quite nice."

The man continued to nod his head and smile. Mao stared at his feet and cleared his throat.

"I, uh, see you did some groceries. I'm off to do some of my own."

Mao stared hard at the bags of beetroot, hoping to get the explanation without having to ask for it. The man didn't seem to notice.

"Oh, yes! Groceries are very nice. Yes! The produce is not as fresh as I am accustomed to, and the people at the store were not as accepting of the way I usually test the quality of the offerings, but certainly the 'supermarket' is a great convenience. Yes? It is much better organized, and so much more hygienic!"

'So much more hygienic than what?' Mao wondered.

Mao couldn't get over the man's voice. In Montréal, one hears a wide range of accents in both English and French... but this one was spoken with the most distinctly musical lilt Mao had ever heard. And he had no idea of its origin.

There was an awkward pause, and Mao made to move past the man, but his massive physique blocked the doorway.

"Lovely day, isn't it?" the man said.

'Lovely day?' Mao took a good look at the man, scanning his face for irony. When he realized there was none to be found, Mao wondered whether the calmness the man emanated could be the product of recreational drug use.

You see, reader, it was November in Montréal, which meant *miserable* weather – rain, snow, or slush, none of which, to Mao anyway, seemed particularly 'lovely'. It was three in the afternoon and the sun was already fading. Mao's instinct, naturally, was that he had misheard, or that the man was pulling his leg. Mao looked at him with a bewildered look on his face, but the man just smiled back earnestly.

"Yes, it is a beautiful, beautiful day."

Mao did his best to keep his voice level.

The man beamed. His teeth were dazzling, like he had just had them bleached and polished. Mao cleared his throat again.

"Well, it was nice meeting you."

Mao offered a nod as he tried once more to move past the man.

"Yes! It was nice to meet you as well! You should come by and see me sometime, young man. If you need help with something, yes, or if you just need someone to talk to?"

The comment startled him and Mao frowned. What was the man suggesting? Why would Mao need to go visit this weirdo to talk? Mao opened his mouth to say something, but thought better of it.

What it had occurred to him to say, and what he might have said, had the man been less huge, was:

'Yeah, I'll give you a call to borrow those robes for Osheaga next year.'

The man continued to stand there with his bags dangerously close to collapse, still blocking the doorway, and watching Mao intently. It seemed to Mao that if he didn't answer him favorably, the towering man wouldn't move. It was like he was face to face with the Sphinx.

"Okay, sure. I might take you up on that."

Mao couldn't quite keep the sarcasm at bay.

"Yes! Good. I think it would be good for you. Yes? I am in Apartment #8 miboy. I will be expecting you."

The man stepped aside. Mao hesitated, worried it might be some kind of trap, and then moved swiftly through the double doors and out into the rain.

'What a strange, troubled young man,' the towering man thought to himself as he watched the younger man scurry away. 'He is just the kind of lonely, lost soul that would benefit from a personal consultation with the Mystic of Mimijad. Yes?'

VIII

In early November, Mao attended a family wedding.

It was a cool and clean afternoon that led into an early sunset, prompting the Ville Émard streetlights to emit their dull incandescent light. The celebration was held in an old church quite remarkably converted into an event venue. The turn of the century stone amplified the sense of romance, and indeed lent an air of timelessness to the joyous occasion. Inside, the venue crackled with the merry din to be expected at one of life's most beautiful rites. The babel was highlighted by the clinking of glasses and the cries of "*Salute!*" or "Cheers!" rising up the hall's high stained-glass walls. At the front, the altar-cum-DJ stage pumped out more or less the songs one expected to hear. The pews, of course, had been removed, and had been replaced with navy blue carpeting under white tables and chairs.

Mao was sitting at one of these white tables, observing the merriment all around him, and yet unable to absorb any of it for himself. He sat surrounded by family, and yet remained, somehow, all alone. His ruminations, unsurprisingly, were centered on a woman. He had initially meant to bring this woman to this wedding... but then, that was no longer in the cards. Mao was giving A–Z the space she had asked for, though it was difficult. He was taking some space for himself and that was a lot easier. It had been over two months since he had seen her. He wasn't too proud to admit that he missed her, a lot, but he was hardheaded enough to bury that burdensome fact under an odd optimism that his state of misery was precisely where he needed to be, creatively. However, in spite of his creatively optimized state of misery, Mao still couldn't write. Well, not with any consistency, anyway. All things considered it seemed to him, sitting there stewing in his misery, that his plan was quite clearly backfiring.

Nevertheless, he had groomed himself nicely, and put his best foot forward. He donned a smile and danced with his mother to Gloria Gaynor's 'I Will Survive' (at her insistence, and much to the enjoyment of his jeering cousins). He ate well, and generally had an okay time without thinking too neurotically about her.

The night dragged on, but Mao managed to get through it with what he felt was admirable composure and grace.

Until, that is, when the end of the night arrived and Mao was making the dutiful rounds of goodbyes. It was in the midst of one of these that a second or third cousin accosted him, with a little bit (a lot) of wine on his breath. This cousin had a rather rotund potbelly bulging out beneath a poorly-judged pinstripe suit, which prompted Mao to wonder why the festively plump always seemed so keen on pinstripe.

The cousin took Mao's hand, but when the time came, wouldn't let it go.

"Hey, you're a writer, right?"

Mao winced.

No because the handshake was too tight, but because this was familiar territory. Mao got it from time to time, and he knew exactly what to expect: unsolicited and probably poor advice. It usually came from the likes of relatives, friends of friends, random bystanders, anyone slightly inebriated, artists who viewed themselves as failures, or, worst of all, people who didn't *personally* read, but nonetheless fancied themselves equipped to straighten out the limp trajectory of his career. They always led in with the same innocuous question:

"Hey, you're a writer, right?"

Mao looked him gingerly in the eyes.

"Oh, uh, yeah. Me. A writer. That's right."

The cousin, whose name Mao could not for the life of him remember, nodded furiously, as though he had been thinking about this for a while.

"Right, right. A writer. So, what are you writing?"

The exaggerated w's whipped unwelcome whiffs of stale wine into the men's bubble of intimacy, beautifully setting the stage for the spit that flies everywhere when one has consumed enough to no longer suffer the inhibitions and tedium of manners. Consciousness of what anyone else thinks or feels is a cage reserved for the sober... and for pussies.

"I'm translating *The Book of Latter Day Saints* into Swahili for my Mormon brothers in Africa."

The cousin's beady eyes widened.

"Oh, wow, no shit?"

Mao cleared his throat.

"It's really challenging, as I do not speak any Swahili. And also as the Mormon church refused to finance the project."

Stripes scrunched his fat face into a frown.

"Hey, you're not messing around with me are you?"

Mao smiled and patted him on the shoulder.

"Yes. I'm sorry. I was only kidding."

Like a toddler discovering his emotions for the first time, the fat man's face slowly brightened.

"Hey, you're funny!"

The two stood there silently a moment.

"So, what are you writing?"

Mao sighed softly.

"I'm working on a novel, sort of."

Mao. So polite. So diplomatic. So stupid.

"Yeah, yeah! A novel. A novel?"

The confused head bobbled affirmatively.

"A novel, yeah. A *novel* novel... about love."

'Hm, that's not so bad,' Mao thought. 'A *novel* novel. I am pretty clever.'

What an idiot.

"Novel novel? About love? Ha, we both know that's not possible!"

The mechanism in the bobbling head switched gears, causing the precariously suspended orb to swing from left to right.

"Not possible?"

Mao was somewhere on the spectrum between amused and crestfallen, which seemed to be his only two moods these days. Engrossed in the talking, swiveling head, he struggled to place the fat man before him somewhere on the spectrum between idiot savant and plain old idiot. He couldn't quite be sure. He couldn't quite be sure of anything, these days.

"That's right. Not possible. It's not possible to write about love in a way that hasn't been done before, or isn't cliché."

'Wow, *negative*,' Mao thought. 'But maybe also a good point?' Mao was taken aback by the sudden lucidity of the morbidly overweight, pinstriped critic. Although he clearly looked ridiculous, he did seem to be making some half decent sense.

"Oh, yeah. Well, I guess that's true."

"Yeah. It is. Trust me."

The cousin looked down into the empty glass that was once filled with wine. Mao turned to leave. The head came shooting back up, and the voice boomed with the faulty volume modulation of the unabashedly drunk.

"A writer, yeah? You know, you're never going to make it."

Amused? Crestfallen? Mao's impulses were divergent.

"Never going to make it? Oh. Why... why is that, do you think?"

Finally, the fat man would prove himself worthy of his stripes. He moved his hands emphatically, theatrically even.

"You can't make it in the arts unless you have pain, tragedy in your life. Bad blood. People who really hate you."

There was a hint of wisdom somewhere in the slurred performance, Mao thought. He frowned, and thought about all of his favorite books. Many of them had been written during or just after World War II. Some were written during the Great Depression, or in the oppressive conditions of Soviet Russia. So many of the books he loved were written in historical periods or social contexts so heavy with strife, and it was undeniable that this was part of what made them so impactful. There was no World War III going on right now, no Great*er* Depression. There was the Internet, and the opioid crisis. There was quantitative easing and fractional reserve banking. There was Netflix and the infinite mediocrity of its infinite content. There were disposable entertainments, and a generation of bored scrolling idiots being passively coerced into who-knows-what.

"Oh, there are people who hate me, I think. As a matter of fact, I'm not a huge fan of myself right now."

The furious head shaking resumed.

"No, no, no. Like, *hate* you. All the best works have that sort of tragic sensibility to them. Your life is too good, kid. You're pampered and soft. You can't be a writer. You should just give up."

Mao thought about this. Although he hated to admit it, everything the fat man said seemed fairly reasonable to him.

"Well, I guess you're right."

The furious nod again.

"Of course I am right. What can you say that hasn't already been said?"

Mao was brainstorming ways of bringing tragedy into his annoyingly level life.

"That hasn't already been said? I'm... not sure."

"Exactly. Not a damn thing. You are incapable of contributing anything original to the world."

The cousin smiled triumphantly. He put his hands on his waist and pulled up his belt. The last few drops of wine spilled out of the glass and onto the navy carpeted floor.

Just then, Mao had an idea.

"Have you, by any chance, read anything I've written?"

And Mao had fallen into the trap. He was supplicating.

"Anything you've written? Oh, I read a few pages."

The cousin was done with the conversation. He had carefully, systematically worn Mao down and earned his emotional-logical checkmate. He had Mao eating out of his pudgy, sausage-fingered hand. There was nothing amusing to him about coddling Mao's fragile ego.

"And?"

The rotund philosopher narrowed his eyes and looked into the distance. He seemed to notice his empty glass again, as though for the first time. He yawned. It was time to return to the bar.

"Your writing? It's alright. Nothing special."

Then, it was Mao who nodded furiously.

"Right, right. Of course not."

IX

Then one day, Mao awoke to find it was December.

On a particularly cold Sunday morning, he woke with a dry mouth and milky vision. As he rubbed his eyes, wondering what he could have done to awake feeling so stiff, he rolled over to politely greet his handheld device on the bedside stand. Groping for the device with only one arm emerging from under the covers, Mao gently maneuvered the screen right up to his squinting eyes. Beyond the periphery of the shining six-inch portal, the old pagan sun persisted, penetrating the room through the slightest slit between the blackout curtains.

Mao unlocked the device, and was pleased to be met with an open file and the blinking cursor of his 'Notes' application. Trailing the blinking cursor, a single written line blinked back at him:

The sadness that arises after sleeping with a stranger.

He put the screen down, and let it all come back slowly.

The night before, he was feeling down. Things were looking bleak, and his emotions had begun to boil over. It was clear A–Z was not coming back to him. She was done, had discarded him for good, leaving him to roam the barren deserts of his soul alone. And so, he wandered. As they often had of late, his wanderings led him to a watering hole only a few blocks away from his apartment building. There, he sat by the dingy bar, and drank. He was thankful for the respite. He was thankful to be alone with his thoughts. After a few drinks, he noticed a girl looking at him inquisitively from across the room, with eyes like glimmering daggers. He could tell immediately that she was several years younger. There was a playful girlishness about her, reserved for the inexperienced. He hadn't yet been with another woman. He approached the glimmering eyes. The girl's demeanor was coy, but receptive. He sat and they drank a little more, together. Much to Mao's surprise, they laughed. Unselfconsciously. She was funny. She was good-natured. After a few rounds, her friends had to go, but she thought she would stay a little while. She didn't live far. It felt comfortable. It felt... easy. He asked her if she wanted to come home with him. In fact, it may have been her idea. Sheltered from the watching eyes of the world, she let herself be taken into his arms. Her skin was soft. His breath was heavy. Her body was eager. His movements were gentle.

When he drove her home later, silently in the earliest hours of the new day, he knew he was not likely to ever see her again. And yet, the fact did not bother him at all.

Driving home, he reckoned with himself. He did not feel any better, but on the other hand, he did not feel any worse. He thought about rock stars, and the way that they continued to sleep with barely legal girls so much longer than most. He reckoned that was what kept them ageless, even as they grew older. That indifference to convention was the fountain of youth, the very center of the universe. He had had a taste, and he wanted another drink. He wanted to be a rock star. He wanted to live that life. And as he pulled up to his apartment building in the early morning, he decided that the small, diamond-hard pit of sadness he felt in the very center of his being was a small fee to pay for entry into the club.

X

Excerpt from Mao's Notes

15/12/2019

THE PRINCE AND THE MAIDEN

Once upon a time, in a kingdom far away, there lived a gallant Prince who, as it appeared to the eyes of the world, had everything a man could want and more. Yet, feeling incomplete, the Prince sought a fair maiden who could love him forevermore and never, ever stray.

At royal functions, ceremonies and banquets, the Prince sought and sought tirelessly for this maiden whom, he believed, would be the one true love to sate his perennial longing.

It was to this end that one fine summer's eve the Prince decided to host a grand castle ball, in the hope of finally encountering this maiden of his visions most ideal, and in time, securing her hand in marriage.

The Prince had held many grand, spectacular balls before, and his servants made the necessary preparations swiftly. The night arrived and the Prince, dressed in his most regal finery, perched himself upon the castle balustrade overlooking the busy ballroom. From his perch, the Prince watched as the dozens of fair young maidens danced in time with the dozens of hardy young men. The Prince quietly observed the valiant men, as one after the other was drawn into the elegant pursuit of his favored damsel. Surveying the familiar scene with disinterest, the Prince's eyes fell upon a figure he was sure he had never seen before. From the moment he laid eyes upon her, whirling to and fro in the arms of some other, lesser man, the Prince became undeniably, and irretrievably smitten.

Who was this beautiful revelation that had swept him away with her beauty and her charm?

As his excitement settled, the Prince became content to observe the maiden patiently, keeping his eyes fixed on her as she graciously accepted dance after dance, with suitor after suitor, entertaining each with her mirth and kindness, while exciting each and all with the lithe, yielding movements of her delicate figure. At length, the Prince could take no more. As the orchestra withdrew for a pause, he hastily descended the long, curving stairway to the ballroom. It took but a moment to pick her out of the crowd, and soon he was standing before her. The Prince stepped to the maiden, and with a warm smile introduced himself, inviting her to share the next dance. The maiden, flattered, graciously obliged. The musicians struck up a waltz, and the two locked in a dancer's embrace. In each other's arms, the pair swayed as synchronous bodies in quintessential counterbalance.

A passionate courtship ensued, and within weeks the two were married in the castle chapel. Their wedding night was everything he had hoped it would be, and the Prince felt, for the first time, as though he was truly happy. In truth, the maiden felt very much the same, and the pair lived happily together for what seemed an eternity.

Until, that is, the Prince began, again, to feel a base, common yearning.

Though he tried and tried, the Prince failed to understand why.

The maiden was fair and graceful as ever, and his passion for her had not waned in the least. Marrying her, as he had believed it would, had eased the painful longing in his soul. Or, at least, it did for a time.

But as the seasons changed, the yearning rising up from deep within the Prince began to stir upon the surface, revealing a passion eerily similar to the longings of his past. Passions, indeed, that the young Prince had thought overcome.

"Why do I feel this way?" the Prince questioned himself in frustration. It had been months, and still the feeling persisted.

Though he did not want to, the Prince could not help but feel that something had been taken from him. He remembered fondly the comfort and ease of his formerly heedless life. Just as he had once longed for the companionship and intimacy that would fill the gaping void in his heart, the Prince now longed for the solitude and abandon that would set his heart free.

Slowly but surely, the innocent maiden's presence began to chafe against the vain Prince's secret desire. Slowly, the proud Prince began to misuse the good maiden. Through acts of conceit, the Prince made the maiden feel by degrees smaller, and less worthy.

Lacking the courage to ask her to leave, the vain Prince wanted to have his cake and eat it too: to keep the good maiden by his side, while simultaneously regaining the princely privilege of his formerly careless life, which was, of course, his birthright. Though the faithful maiden did whatever she could to appease him, the callow Prince pushed and pushed her away, until the gentle maiden dangled over the abyss at the very end of her rope. Though she could not deny her love for the Prince, she had come to terms with the fact that he no longer made her happy. The Prince had left her no choice but to flee the castle. And this she did, back to her village in the foothills of the kingdom.

Knowing he was to blame, the Prince let her go.

The seasons once again were swept away, and the former lovers grew apart.

The maiden eased back into her life in the village. She had missed her family and loved ones. She rekindled lost and neglected relationships, as she rewove herself into the fabric of her former life. The Prince, on the other hand, spent much of his time indulging in the ephemeral pleasures of his princely estate, and the rest of it brooding in the solitude of the castle tower.

Though he missed her, and she missed him, neither of them understood what could, or should be done about it. In the seclusion of the tower, the petty Prince struggled to accept that the maiden once his, was no longer. Time passed and the Prince's brooding turned to bitterness, as his heart became hardened with regret. Bitterness fomented his pride, and the Prince's rash temperament began to flare.

Eventually, a time came when the Prince could take no more. Though he knew no good could come of it, he stole away on horseback, riding fiercely into the nearest village. There, in the seediest tavern, he sought out disreputable men eager to dirty their hands in exchange for gold. Settled at a darkened table with a flagon of ale, the Prince dropped a heavy sack upon the table before a band of hooded men. The gold was counted, and a pact was made. These dangerous men he took under his employ, charging them to find his lost maiden, to follow her, and to bring back the tidings of all they would find.

"I must know if my maiden has remained faithful to me," the faithless Prince cried.

The hooded men asked few questions, and did as they were told. Indeed they did so gladly, for they were rewarded handsomely in gold. They sought far and wide for the maiden, whom the arrogant Prince believed was his alone. They searched and they searched, on behalf of the corrupt heir to the throne.

Eventually, the men found the maiden's village in the foothills at the very end of the kingdom, where she had finally found peace among her kindred. The hooded men settled into the village as weary travellers seeking respite, and watched the fair maiden for three days and three nights. It was on the third of these unhappy nights that it so happened the maiden would attend a ball.

Following behind, the hooded men watched from the shadows as the maiden laughed and danced unselfconsciously, just as she had done all those years ago. The maiden was fair and graceful as ever, and still attracted an array of suitors who vied for her affection. Although, as the hooded men were sure to note, there was one suitor alone who left with the maiden on his arm, at the end of the ball.

With this intelligence, the hooded men hastily returned to the Prince who awaited their return in the tower. "My Prince, we found the maiden!" the hooded men exclaimed. "Tell me everything, and leave nothing out," the Prince impetuously demanded. The men did as they were told, but not before the Prince handed them the ransom of gold that sealed their bond, and sealed his fate.

The news of the maiden's new suitor shattered the Prince's fragile hopes, maiming him as though a dagger had been ruthlessly plunged through his heart. The Prince reviewed the details as he paced the castle, plunging himself deeper and deeper into the depths of obsession and despair.

Before the seasons could change once more, the Prince's bitterness had turned his heart entirely to stone. Until the day came when he could no longer take the pain.

In a fit of madness spurred by the unrelenting melancholy of his shameful discovery, the Prince stole away once more on the back of his swiftest steed, making for the foothills where he hoped his maiden might still be. Galloping into the village as quickly as the beast's legs would carry him, the Prince arrived at last at the maiden's home. Knocking at the humble door of the humble stone house in a fury, the maiden at last appeared upon the threshold.

Faced with her beauty and grace for the first time in years, the Prince was stricken as by lightning upon the highest node, bewildered by the full realization of all that he had lost. As he gazed into her gentle eyes after all this time, the Prince saw a face that looked at once familiar, yet somehow also heartbreakingly remote.

Though it had proven a long journey for her, the maiden stood before him in the radiance and glory of a being truly at peace.

Stunned by the irreverence of the maiden's independence, the Prince lunged forward, grabbing at the maiden's hands with an urgency that immediately betrayed his madness. Though the maiden had long dreamt of the moment she and the Prince might finally meet again, now that he was here before her in this crazed and desperate state, she could not help but shudder in revolt. The maiden took one glance at the Prince, and saw not the man she had once known and loved, but instead a vile, wicked spirit, debased beyond salvation.

Noticing how the maiden shriveled away from his embrace, the Prince made one last anguished attempt to change her mind, to undo what he had done, and to resurrect the spectral memories he had preserved in his tower of solitude for so long.

But the maiden was resolute.

She had lived so long without the Prince, and she was now decidedly happier without him.

The Prince nodded his head weakly. There was nothing more he could say. He understood this was the end. It was just as he was turning to leave, however, that a man emerged from the depths of the stone house, joining the maiden at the threshold. Looking upon his face, the Prince recognized the ungainly suitor as the lesser man who had danced with his maiden at his grand castle ball, what seemed like a lifetime ago.

As the recognition settled in, the curtains began to close on the Prince's tragic fate. Drawing his dagger from its sheath, the Prince held it up to the light of midday. Then, looking his love in the eyes, he plunged the dagger straight into his heart. The maiden's eyes widened in horror as the Prince dropped to his knees, and groaned his parting words:

"This is what you did to me. You put this dagger through my heart.

Now, with all this blood on your hands, we will never be apart."

And with that, the Prince fell to the ground and perished, leaving the maiden behind to suffer for what she did to him. Though she had never admitted it to herself, the maiden suddenly realized that her new suitor had proven a futile effort to forget her love for the Prince. The maiden felt a crippling guilt about her new suitor, and about her supposed crime.

In time, the seasons changed again, and slowly, the maiden healed. It took her some time, but with enough patience and grace she eventually came to realize the truth that the Prince had not. It was this undeniable truth that ultimately gave her the courage to let go of the past and set herself free.

The truth was simply this: it was the Prince himself, and not the maiden, who had driven the dagger through his heart.

XI

Ricardo gently lowered the stack of ruffled papers onto the granite tabletop, and looked up to meet Mao's eager, waiting eyes. Ricardo cleared his throat.

"Well, first of all, I'm impressed."

Mao leaned back in his chair. A relieved smile brightened his face, and he exhaled.

"Really?"

Ricardo grinned.

"Really. That read like, like it was written by a true lord."

A lord! Mao was over the moon. He was really nervous about what Ricardo would think of the piece. He knew it was a little different, stylistically, and a little sensitive. It wasn't the kind of thing he usually shared with anyone. Or, at least, definitely not with anyone like Ricardo.

"Rick, I can't tell you how glad I am to hear that. That's definitely the style I was going for. Like a medieval, romantic kind of thing, you know?"

Mao smiled across the table at him, and Ricardo smiled back widely.

"Well, you definitely nailed it, buddy. There's no doubt in my mind that the piece was written by a legitimate Gaylord."

Ricardo let the comment sit, savoring the grotesque contortion of Mao's face as his heart sank. Ricardo, on the other hand, was effervescent. Watching Mao shake his head, Ricardo smiled at him like a shit-flinging monkey, and when he finally burst, his laughter resonated even over the din of the busy restaurant. Mao rubbed his temples.

"It's 2019, you philistine. That's not right. You can't say stuff like that anymore. Never mind that your comment even without the slur is in bad taste."

Ricardo laughed some more before eventually settling down. He wiped the tears from his eyes with his napkin, gathered himself, and then sassily raised an eyebrow. He leaned forward, resting an elbow on the table and letting his chin fall into the open palm of his hand.

"Sweetheart, please. If you really want to turn this moment into a stand for social justice, you know what would actually make a difference? You could go home, make sure to lube yourself up real well, find yourself a nice, smooth cucumber..."

"Alright, alright, alright. Enough."

Mao tried, but there was no stopping Ricardo when he had this kind of momentum.

"Oh, you knew where I was going with that, did you? Clever boy. Well, you try it out and let me know. Your tightly-clenched virgin cheeks will thank me later."

Ricardo winked lewdly.

"In fact, hon, I'm so confident they will, I can wait here while you go home, and then come back to tell me how much you enjoyed it. Go ahead. Please, I insist! No? Not interested in giving it a whirl? Well, then, perhaps you shouldn't fuss too much over the words I use. As a writer, I really thought you'd have a better understanding of the word 'irony'."

Ricardo's stare was a challenge. Mao shrugged it off. He didn't want to get into this argument with Ricardo. There was no winning. He looked down at the folded manuscript resting on the table between them. Upon being seated, the men had asked for a moment of privacy, but the waitress ought to have brought the menus over by now.

Mao had a hunch that Ricardo would hate the piece, but he didn't think he'd be such a bully about it. Ricardo was, well, Ricardo was a special case. To put it bluntly: he was a crass, sexually depraved animal. He was a brute, a horn dog, a deviant with no interest in culture, albeit an avowed enthusiasm for curvature. He was, after all, bisexual. What's more, he was bisexual in an age and society more overtly accepting and curious about the mysteries of sexuality than any had ever been before. Ricardo, an admittedly handsome, well-off, and reasonably articulate man — well, it was clear he would have no shortage of 'opportunities'. Men and women: everyone was in play. The whole world was a sexual buffet to him, of the all-you-can-eat variety. Though, the funny thing was that no matter how much he ate, Ricardo always seemed to have room for more. Never starving, but always hungry. Always interested in eating for the sake of eating. A glutton. A big, fat, sexual glutton.

Obviously, there was no way a person like that could appreciate the subtlety and sensitivity of Mao's work.

"Using gay slurs is not ironic, Rick. It's lazy. I know you can do better."

Mao was admittedly mad at himself. You see, he didn't actually care about the stupidity coming out of Ricardo's mouth. Ricardo spewing stupidity: that was nothing new. He had to be willing to humor some spewage if he was planning on indulging Ricardo's company. It was just that, balanced and objective reader, Mao hadn't expected that Ricardo would actually read the whole piece. Any way Mao sliced it, that fact was pretty damning. You see, it was one thing to dismiss something offhand, based on a short description of the thing, or because the person recommending had a history of dubious recommendations. But it was a whole other thing to read a piece from start to finish, gather your thoughts, and then dismiss it. Rick was still grinning across the table, making a veritable feast of Mao's sour grapes.

"Listen, Mao, you've got to get with the times. When I tell people I enjoy butt play, and believe me, I do not hesitate to share, I know you won't believe it, but these days, they let me skip to the front of the line! I was used to that kind of thing happening from time to time at the club, where the name of the game was depravity, but now it works," Ricardo lowered his voice here, "*even at the grocery store.* I'm telling you! I promise, it's true. They don't know what to do with it. One second we're in the middle of civil discourse about how to pick out a good watermelon, and the next there I am casually espousing the nuanced benefits anal beads. Mao, you've got to see it! The straights have absolutely no idea what to do with it. They get all flustered, and say something stupid like 'oh, of course! My nephew's a homosexual', or 'I couldn't agree more! I'm a progressive, you know', and then they let me skip ahead of them to the brain dead teenager at the register. It's a brave new world out there, Mao. And you know what? You need to check your privilege, cupcake. *You,*" Ricardo pointed fiercely here, sprinkling just the right amount of venom into his voice, "*a straight white male,* cannot tell *me* what I can and cannot say. It's the twenty-first century, baby doll, and *I* am a liberated gay man. I can say whatever the hell I want, whenever the hell I want, and really, it's about damn time!"

Mao rolled his eyes, but couldn't help but grin. A liberated gay man... as if. It wasn't that Ricardo didn't enjoy sex with men, he did. Mao had endured many a graphic tale, and every single one as detailed as it was unsolicited, mind you. The thing was that Ricardo didn't enjoy sex with *just* men. He was partial towards pretty much any kind of friction. Mao liked to believe Ricardo drew the line at humans, or at least at bipeds, but there was as of yet no concrete evidence going either way. The whole 'liberated gay man' routine was just the shtick he used to get away with his terrible manners. He identified as gay when it was convenient, when he could get something out of it. When there was a hot chick around that he wanted to bone, he somehow always managed to omit the little detail that he liked, and very possibly even preferred the other team's equipment. Even when the guy was caught in his doubletalk (Ricardo, as one of God's many creations with very little self-control, was known to regularly flirt with both the most attractive man *and* the most attractive woman in any given room, which naturally led, from time to time, to his hypothetical Johnsons getting tangled), the most Mao had ever heard him concede was that he was 'just ever so mildly bi-curious'. 'Gay man, my ass,' Mao thought, and then sighed at what Freud might have deemed a slip. The point was that the man was a rapscallion! And a double agent! Both sides were being played against the other. Why, the smug bastard ought to be castrated for his treachery and –

Mao's thoughts were interrupted by Ricardo's elbows hitting the table again, as he brought the manuscript up to his face where he could examine it more carefully. Mao bit his thumb.

"Was it really *that* bad?" he asked anxiously, hating himself for it.

Ricardo didn't answer right away. He looked the last page over, nodded, sighed, and then tossed the small stack of papers across the smooth granite tabletop at Mao.

"Babe, I gotta be straight with you. That is some of the vilest smut that I have ever read. And that's coming from me."

Mao couldn't help letting out a sigh.

It was only one o'clock in the afternoon, but the place was full. The bistro, though small, was clamorous with the clinks and clacks of silverware on porcelain, and the mirthful chatter characteristic of a Friday afternoon in Montréal. The atmosphere was resplendent with the smell of tartare, French fries and coarse salt. The men were dressed cleanly but casually, having come directly from the gym. Ricardo was in jeans and a black short-sleeved shirt, characteristically designer, and characteristically tighter than anything Mao would ever consider wearing. Mao was in jeans and his favorite band tee. Ricardo ran one of his hands through his slick black hair, lifted his chin and looked down the ridge of his slender nose at Mao.

"Darling, you know what? You need to hear this. I was being understated. That thing you brought for me to read, it was worse than terrible. It was pathetic. One, two, three. You hear that? *Pa-the-tic.* It is a smoldering heap of dog shit. You can never show that to anyone again. Alright? I forbid you. That garbage will be the end of you."

'Does he mean steaming? Why in the hell would a heap of dog shit ever be smoldering?' Mao wondered. He hated it when Ricardo called him 'babe', or 'hon' or whatever the hell his flavor of the week derogatory term was. The worst one of them all was 'doll'. What was especially annoying was that when Ricardo invoked those terms – the cocked weapons in the verbal arsenal of this 'liberated gay man'– it was usually right before he got derisive, or overly animated about something entirely irrelevant. Ricardo, who was watching Mao suspiciously, paused for a moment to steal a crisp glance at his watch, and to follow that up with a yawn. He went on:

"Give it to me and I'll burn it. I'm telling you, it's for your own good."

Mao thought it better not to reply.

If you have nothing good to say...

...don't tell the other guy what he's saying is a smoldering heap of dog shit.

In the ensuing uncomfortable silence, Ricardo began to fidget with his fork.

"This is unbelievable. I have to get back to the gym soon. My lunch break is almost over, and our order hasn't even been taken yet. This place is a mess. Why did we come here?"

'Here' was *Pince*, the latest trend on the Montréal restaurant scene, and the new crown jewel of Rue Saint Denis. Though the service was incredibly slow, *Pince*, it must be stated, was at the very least exquisitely decorated. It exuded a turn-of-the-century Parisian vibe, fortified by a few decorative rotary phones, ornate ridge-backed chairs, a granite bar, those small, circular café-style tables, several antique gilded mirrors hung up on the walls, and an array of plants sprouting out of terracotta pots seemingly everywhere. However, it was the cramped seating arrangement and profanely expensive menu that really inspired the bistro's name. Or, at least, that was Mao's little joke. *Pince* was a small locale, serving only twenty or so small tables at maximum capacity. It was always at maximum capacity, of course, and in its signature style, there was always just one waitress working.

Woah, woah, woah. Time out. Wait a minute. How in the world could poor old Mao be eating at such a place? Could he ever afford such a thing? you might be asking yourself, if you are a clever little boy, or girl, or boygirl, or girlboy, or tomboy, or boy shaped android, or talking animal partial to boys, haha, just kidding, that's not a very nice way to talk about Catholic priests, or even if you are simply a gaseous cloud of asexual sentience who has suddenly remembered that we previously described Mao's socio-economic status as somewhere in the neighborhood of pitiful. Well, you nosy little reader whose cute little cheeks we would love to pinch (we mean that in the most non-Catholic way possible), the truth is that he could *not* afford to be eating at such a place. The simple fact, cherished one, was that Mao never, ever picked up the cheque when Ricardo invited him to lunch. We figure this may clear some things up about the dynamic at play in this feature. To be clear, Ricardo's generosity was one of the only reasons Mao agreed to go to lunch with him at all. He had tried to get out of it many times, but the man was persistent! As to his motives, well, Mao was willing to turn a blind eye. Or, at least, a partially blind eye. Mao just made sure Ricardo never handled any of his drinks.

Now, before you go off thinking that Mao was just as depraved as Ricardo, or that he was a cheapskate and/or a leech on society, let us clarify. The absolutely singular phenomenon of Mao never picking up the cheque while in the presence of Ricardo was partially, yes *partially*, explained by the fact that Ricardo had obscenely expensive taste. Oh, yes. He did. Furthermore, Ricardo was always extremely adamant about choosing the restaurant or bar he and Mao must go to. He was inviting! He insisted. Mao's protests were futile. So, whenever he was with Ricardo, Mao was forced *against his will* to go somewhere he could not afford to go otherwise. Thus, it was only natural that Ricardo would pick up the cheque.

There, isn't that a reasonable rationalization?

Explanation.

We meant explanation.

Ricardo was about ten years older than Mao, and very successful. What kind of successful? Ricardo looked through the windshield of his Maserati from behind his Gucci sunglasses. His entire wardrobe was made of imported fabrics and bespoke. He kept in very, very good shape. In a word, Ricardo took great pains to look his best. He was one of those slightly annoying 'mindset' people who were always mouthing off about self-improvement, meditation, and their mottos. Ricardo's favorite was 'look good, feel good.' Nothing groundbreaking, sure, but as far as mottos go, we'll concede it was moderately workable.

Ricardo owned the gym Mao frequented. In fact, that was where they met. Ricardo had taken a liking to Mao from the first time they met at 'Fit for Eternity'. The gym was located not too far from Mao's apartment, on Saint Laurent Street facing Jarry Park. 'Fit for Eternity', of course, is not to be confused with Ricardo's two other gyms, 'Turbo Pump' in the West Island, and the highly successful 'Kosher Beast' in Outremont (whose neon signage features a buff, Kippah-wearing bulldog doing bicep curls in space). 'Fit for Eternity' is also not to be confused with Ricardo's (now infamous) failed venture, the 'Muscle Church' development in the Mile End, which, as anyone 'in the know' will tell you, was driven to bankruptcy because the denizens of the Mile End borough ironically mistook the dubiously branded 'Muscle Church' for a branch of the Holy Church of Scientology. In our opinion, the place was doomed to fail from the start anyhow, because the tarts and libertines who live in the Mile End are equally allergic to both religion *and* muscle tone.

It is a cardinal mistake, in both art and in business, to misread your audience.

Anyway, Ricardo, who often made friends with the jocks and juice heads who frequented his establishments, thought he saw a glimmer of his younger, once idealistic self in Mao's earnest, wandering eyes. The story was basically like this: at the gym one day, Mao was trying to bench more weight than he could, and without a spotter at that, and he wasn't seeing the kind of success he had hoped for (something of a motif, isn't it?). In fact, Mao was on the verge of some pretty serious physical and emotional damage when Ricardo, who often took breaks from his paperwork to get some reps in and maintain his own eternal pump, gallantly stepped in to help ensure that the two-hundred-pound barbell did not decapitate our red-faced hero on that fateful day. Mao thanked him profusely as he caught his breath, and Ricardo laughed at him good-naturedly. When Mao could stand up straight, he introduced himself and the men exchanged a firm shake.

The rest, as they say, is history.

Yes, *his*tory, and not *her*story.

Because this one, dear reader, was a bromance at first lift.

The pair quickly became gym buddies. Upon discovering that they were both bachelors, Ricardo suggested that they go 'cruising' together. Evidently, in this case, Ricardo had not yet introduced himself as a 'liberated gay man', and so there were a few early bumps in the road the two needed to work out before they made it onto the same page. Eventually, though, the two got pretty tight. Ricardo began inviting Mao to lunch from time to time, after his workout. Mao, who rarely had anything better to do with his Friday afternoons, often accepted the invitation. Mao enjoyed Ricardo's older, occasionally wiser perspective, and of course his generosity. Ricardo enjoyed Mao's youthful innocence (or ignorance), and his willingness to make a fool of himself. Mao viewed Ricardo as a mentor (in a very limited sense). Ricardo viewed Mao as entertainment (in a very broad sense). Although the only things they had in common were that they were single and worked out, they found a way to make it work.

Men are simple like that.

Anyway, we got a little carried away again. Fate works in mysterious ways, we suppose. One might think that Fate would work in a linear, clearly defined way, but that isn't the case. We're as scatter-brained and haphazard as a pipe-smoking monkey, and only half as intelligent! But, that is beside the point. The point is, reader, that Ricardo *always* picked up the bill, and that is the main reason why it makes sense that this conversation would be staged at a place like *Pince,* alright?

"You picked the place, buddy."

Mao emphatically stated the obvious. Ricardo narrowed his eyes, annoyed. He didn't like it when Mao got cheeky with him, especially since it wasn't lost on him that he always picked up the cheque.

"Yeah, well. I've been told the food is to die for, if you manage to get it before you actually die of old age."

Mao chuckled perfunctorily. It was the least he could do to laugh at Ricardo's lame jokes. Ricardo had only two gears: wildly inappropriate and dad joke. Ricardo turned away, trying to make eye contact with the waitress, like everyone else in the place. Mao looked over, too, and noticed that the waitress was a strikingly pretty blonde in the full bloom of her early twenties. Ricardo's eyes were locked onto her like lasers. The waitress, however, was working the orders for another table.

Mao sighed. He wasn't pressed for time. He watched the young waitress at work. She looked a little overwhelmed by the crowded dining room. Scrutinizing her, Mao wondered if it was true that beautiful women always felt the eyes of men on them, as though through a keen sixth sense. What did they call that in the seminars? *The Male Gaze.* He wondered what that might be like, to be coveted or admired by everyone without doing a damn thing, and wherever you went. It sounded both thrilling and tiresome.

While Ricardo's gaze conveyed the urgency of his biological demand for nourishment, Mao's was disinterested and languid, at ease in the contemplation of the pretty waitress, as though in passive appreciation of a wildflower bending to the meadow's gentle breeze. There was something so inherently appealing about a beautiful waitress, wasn't there? There was something about the paradigm that touched upon an unaccountable madness he recognized somewhere deep in his gut. Watching the beautiful girl rush to and fro in her white blouse and black skirt, with the notepad in her breast pocket always at an arm's reach, her hair a bit of a mess, laying plates down a few tables over only to rush back through the swinging doors of the kitchen for some more, was like cutting himself open and searching his entrails for something he always suspected was there, but had never seen.

The thought intrigued him. He tried to follow it, to capture it, and to disfigure it by forcing it into words.

It wasn't just that she was a beautiful young woman, though that in and of itself was normally enough to soften him up to contemplation of the sublime. It was that the vixen's delicate beauty was being eroded through both the passing of time, and her subjection to hard work. It seemed so grotesque that this beautiful creature should be toiling, harder than she wanted to no doubt, and at something she clearly disliked. She was sweating, and she looked flustered. She was overwhelmed and in distress. She looked so miserable, and yet so simultaneously full of a redeemable vitality. She was just that: an elegant wildflower, tragically misplaced.

And it could all so easily be righted. With a few simple changes, everything could be fixed. It could all so easily be corrected. She could be so easily... *saved.*

Bingo.

The blinking lights went off in Mao's head.

'The modern day's closest equivalent to the damsel awaiting her knight in shining armor, and I'm just the kind of jackass who would give his left testicle to face the mighty dragon and defend my lady's honor,' Mao thought. 'A closeted romantic, turned bitter by my fantasies of, what?' He gathered the little heap of papers in front of him, and squared them with a tap on the table.

"Well, thanks for reading the piece anyway, Rick. I knew I could count on you to be honest with me."

Mao leaned down and stashed the papers in his messenger bag, then tucked it away under his tiny, uncomfortable chair.

Ricardo paid him no mind. Though really, Mao didn't care. There was nothing more to say about the piece, especially after Ricardo's blunt reaction to it. He just needed to forget about it. Chalk it up to bad judgment, that's all. It happens. Pick yourself up, dust yourself off, and try again.

Before being seated, the pair had to wait a little while in line. It was cold, but when they finally got inside, the men were lucky enough to be seated by a window. Looking out that window, Mao was thrilled to have a view of the street. The busy thoroughfare was always adorned with festive lights this time of year. Rue Saint Denis was peppered with storefronts and restaurants, and they generated foot traffic all year round. Because of this, Rue Saint

The Cliché

Denis was one of Mao's favorite areas to people-watch in all of Montréal.

In the world just beyond the glass, snow had recently begun to fall. Mao watched the thick clumps slowly drifting to the ground, softly enveloping the city in a fluffy white embrace. Though it always happened gently and by degrees, the end result was always the same: the city succumbed to nature's will and went white.

The piece he had shown Ricardo had come to him on a whim, like everything he had been writing lately. Nothing at all about anything he was producing seemed deliberate to him, all of his work of late amounting to a big disorganized mess. This piece, the one he had shown Ricardo, he had at least reworked a few times. Which was more than he could say for the majority of the ideas he would begin to draft, only to abandon. Contrary to popular belief, that was not how things worked: no writer drafted genius. A writer drafted, and then edited, and then revisited, reconsidered, and edited some more. Though for Mao, the drafting was likely the hardest, or at least the most elusive part of the writing process. It was the first step, the conquering of the frontier. It was a boxing match with the blank page. Drafting necessitated the hardest work: the work of drawing at the well of 'inspiration', and the work of drinking the mystic water down quickly, before it could slip through one's fingers. The well was universally acknowledged to exist somewhere, in some way, though it remained as of yet undetectable by even the most sophisticated machinery. However, it was during the editing part of the process that the majority of the magic happened. No writer drafted genius. Most drafted verbal diarrhea. The genius emerged from a process of sharpening or cleaning, as though a razor run over and over against a strop, or to put the analogy in Canadian terms, as though a Zamboni passing over a sheet of ice, with each pass cleaning, leveling, and perfecting the ice until even the most fastidious skater would be salivating for a chance to glide along its smooth surface. Until that skater, or reader was salivating, genius had yet to be achieved. Such was the process of writing. Though for whatever reason, Mao's Zamboni was still broken. Perhaps the driver had gone on strike. And so, not only were the drafts he wrote haphazard and meaningless, they were dirty, because Mao was unwilling to do the dirty work of imbuing them with meaning.

Mao knew that there was still something wrong with the piece he had shown Ricardo, but he couldn't put his finger on it. That's why he shouldn't have shown it to anyone. It wasn't ready. But then, maybe Ricardo might have been able to offer some insight into what was missing. Wasn't that the idea? The creative principle was that different perspectives were good, right? Mao glanced over at Ricardo's intricate hairdo, down to the long gold chain dangling around his neck, up his tattooed arms to his bulging, vascular biceps.

He sighed.

He knew he was grasping at straws.

Mao looked out into the world of white and tried to clear his mind. Maybe it was that the piece was too... sensitive? No. That made no sense. Sensitive wasn't the word. Sensitive would be fine. Sensitive would be good, even. Yes, sensitive was something a writer wanted. That wasn't it. It was that it was... it's that it was... what was it!

Ah, yes.

Masochistic.

Capital M.

That was the one, and it was always going to be a problem.

If he was dead-set on showing someone the piece, and so revealing his *masochism,* of all people he should not have revealed it to Ricardo. He should have waited until he had the chance to show it to one of his female friends, or someone a little less blunt. Perhaps someone with a little more tact. Then again, maybe he should have just deleted it. Then again, again, why would he show it to anyone who wasn't capable of being blunt? He didn't want to be taken for a ride, did he? This wasn't his first rodeo.

Then again once more, Ricardo was just a meathead. He was a macho man, a crude, primitive beast, a mindless ape! He wasn't sophisticated enough to discuss art. He hadn't the faintest about matters of the heart. The guy was six-three, jacked, and wore tight t-shirts that accentuated the tattoos running up and down both his arms. He sported the type of *coup sauvage* favored by vain sociopaths of only the highest order: the ones who spent hundreds, if not thousands of dollars on hair products every year. He bleached his teeth and probably other orifices. He was perpetually tan. In Montréal, where it was sunny two months out of the year! He wore garish rings and used the word 'bro' with impunity.

You get it.

Ricardo had recently gotten out of a short relationship with a man (a doomed attempt at monogamy), and Mao suspected he was just the slightest bit bitter about it. Although, Mao may have just been projecting his own feelings.

Ricardo's foot was tapping anxiously against the floor, and he had begun to whistle. Mao looked across the room, and saw that the poor waitress was slowly making her way to their side of the dining room, systematically taking orders and scribbling furiously on her little pad. Mao watched an elderly couple a few tables over devouring their hamburgers with gusto, and realized he, too, was hungry.

The bottom line was that Mao just needed to show someone his work for the sake of showing someone his work, you know? It was important for a writer to share his work, to overcome the fear of exposure that lingers when one hoards one's writing for only one's self, or perhaps for a select few who would never honestly criticize it. To operate that way would be absolute creative death.

"What was wrong with it, Rick?"

Ricardo had gotten the waitress' attention, and was smiling at her and winking. She smiled back, and what a smile it was! She gave the sign that she would be over shortly.

Without missing a beat, Ricardo turned to face Mao and shook his head firmly.

"That thing you made me read? I'll tell you exactly what was wrong with it. Very simple: too soft, bro."

The offhand nature of the comment annoyed Mao, though he did his best not to show it. He wanted to hear Ricardo out, to find a way to access the seemingly impenetrable complexity of his worldview. However much Mao wanted to mock his simplemindedness, Ricardo *was* highly successful. In money and in mating. These facts were undeniable. According to Mao's beliefs, that meant there had to be something to Ricardo's *modus operandi*, right? It couldn't just be *all* dumb luck, could it?

"Yeah, alright. Unpack that. Tell me what you mean."

Ricardo looked at Mao, and nodded. He leaned forward, his massive frame towering over the little tabletop. He looked like a monster at some dainty, demented tea party. Mao could have laughed in Ricardo's face, had the circumstances been different.

The man was picking up the cheque after all.

"You need me to spell it out for you, bro?"

Mao smirked.

"You know how to spell?"

Ricardo didn't blink. Mao rolled his eyes.

"Yes, please. Spell it out for me professor."

Ricardo nodded.

"It's like I said, babe. It was soft. The thing had no balls. Not relatable at all."

Ricardo was relishing this new role of art critic. He ran his hand through his stupid hair and looked off into the distance, as though he was contemplating the profundity of his comments. Based on the face he was making, one would have thought Ricardo had just confirmed the existence of God.

'What a meathead!' Mao thought as he ground his teeth. Mao could have punched Ricardo straight in his stupid face, if it wasn't for the fact that Ricardo would have easily beaten the living daylights out of him, and more importantly, that Mao would then probably also be left with the cheque.

"Alright, bud, thank you for the input. It's very illuminating and all, but again, please tell me what you mean by that. You said it wasn't relatable. Why wasn't it relatable?"

Ricardo was loving it. It was not their conventional dynamic that Mao would be lapping up Ricardo's opinions about art. Mao valued Ricardo's opinions about squats and intermittent fasting, certainly, but not about art. Not about his writing. Not until this moment, anyway. Ricardo was drinking it up like a fine vintage, maximizing this rare opportunity to unleash the full power of his inner art snob.

"It's way too feminine, bro. The main character is just a little bitch. I simply cannot associate."

Mao really thought about this. Ricardo was a total moron, that was certain, and he wasn't Mao's implied reader, that was also true, but none of that implicitly invalidated the points he was making.

"Okay, the main character is a little bitch. I think I get it. Can you tell me a little more? Why is he a bitch?"

Mao checked the impulse to reach into his bag for a pen and paper for notes, and a good thing, too. That would have really gotten Ricardo going. If Ricardo saw Mao with a pen poised to paper and hanging on his every word, Mao would never live something like that down. After something like that, Ricardo (who was already very generous with his spare change) would be offering his unsolicited two cents about everything and anything Mao did. He'd start offering Mao advice about what boxers to wear. He'd start offering advice about what kind of coffee beans he should be drinking in the morning. He'd start offering advice about every aspect of Mao's writing career, the fact that he had never successfully read a book notwithstanding. Hell, eventually Ricardo would realize that Mao was just an impediment, and that he, Ricardo, had been the true literary genius all along. Pretty soon, Mao would be helping Ricardo compile his priceless pearls of wisdom for their eventual publication by Penguin Random House. Mao could see it: *Meditations of a Meathead: The Alpha*

Peabrain's Handbook for Daily Living. The cover art would be a waist up shot of Ricardo in a tiny white t-shirt, with his Gucci sunglasses on and his tattooed arms folded in the expert's power pose.

No. Mao wasn't going down that road. He'd jump into the rails at Berri-UQAM before he lived to see that nightmare materialize.

No notes.

Ricardo let his head and shoulders fall, as if the answer to Mao's question was so exasperatingly obvious and Mao was just an absolute tool for even asking.

"Bro, the prince killed himself over some broad? *C'mon, bro.* The guy was the prince."

Ricardo tilted his head to the side. Mao stared earnestly at him.

"I'm not sure that I follow."

Ricardo frowned and put a finger to his temple.

"Are you serious, bro? The guy was the *prince*! Do you even understand what kind of access a guy like that would have? He'd be drenched in a tsunami of punani every time he stepped outside the castle. Broads would constantly be throwing their pussies at him! You remember that Eddie Murphy bit in *Delirious?* When Eddie became so famous and had so much pussy being thrown at him, it would be falling out of his pockets as he walked down the street? And he was just a comedian! I can't even imagine the sea of hoo-hah that a *prince* would be able to part."

Mao raised his eyebrows in surprise. Ricardo, in his lift-things-up-and-put-them-down, blunt-force-trauma kind of way, was actually making a good bit of sense.

"If I recall, our rambunctious prince threw a party to find the first woman, correct?"

"Yeah. He did."

Ricardo made a sarcastic face.

"So? Why the hell wouldn't he just throw another party to find another? And the next one after that? What, was Junior out of money all of a sudden? Or, did he stop working out, bro?"

Ricardo was working himself up, setting Mao up for the finish. Mao played along, smirking.

"No. Junior was not out of money, and he did not stop working out."

Ricardo slapped the tabletop, rattling the cutlery.

"No kidding! And that, that's why it doesn't make any sense. None whatsoever. Complete waste of time."

Mao grimaced playfully at Ricardo, egging him on.

"No sense, huh?"

Ricardo had a full head of steam.

"Total stupidity! The guy's a young millionaire, in shape, and, wait, his dick still works, right?"

Mao chuckled.

"Right."

"Right! Perfectly! And yet, he's worrying for years and years about some broad from a hick village in the hills? *C'mon, bro.* Would never happen. And if it did, we circle back to my original point, which was screw that guy, he's a bitch!"

Though he couldn't help the smile on his face, Mao was letting it all sink in. Ricardo's logic, though deeply rooted in Neanderthal principles, seemed to him, nonetheless, irrefutably illuminating. Perhaps he had not sufficiently thought through his character's motives.

Ricardo stole another glance at his watch. Little beads of sweat were beginning to form at the hairline, and the vein in his temple was pulsing.

"Besides, who's the prince supposed to be, huh? You? Because let me tell you buddy, you don't look like any prince to me."

Mao laughed good-naturedly. He realized he was being mocked, and that by locker room rules he was meant to retaliate with a ribbing of his own. However, he didn't have it in him. The truth was that although he was highly entertained, Mao was also simultaneously in awe of Ricardo. There was something about Ricardo's conviction that was so undeniably compelling. It was like Ricardo was so certain of himself that reality became secondary to his conviction, and so would naturally bend to his will.

What a revelation!

What *masculinity!*

"Why are you writing that filth, anyway? It's morbid. Actually, why am I asking silly questions? I know why. The real question is, when's the last time you got laid, babe?"

Ricardo was outright belittling him now, and getting a little bit nasty. But Mao didn't mind. He was laughing, and still seriously considering whether it could be that Ricardo was at once troglodyte *and* trailblazer.

"Yeah, it's been a little while. I don't know Rick. Why did I write that? I guess I've just been feeling a little down about the breakup. Trying to express myself, you know? It doesn't always come out right."

Ricardo leaned over so that the tiny table was completely eclipsed by that massive frame of his, forever challenging the structural integrity of the size small shirts he forced across its expanse. Ricardo spoke softly, and with what seemed to be his best attempt to convey sympathy. The man wasn't used to this type of sentimentality, and so his delivery may have come off a little labored, or a little laden with homicidal tendencies, but we can tell you for sure he genuinely meant well.

"Look, bro, you know I love you. You best believe that's true, otherwise there would be no reason for me to put up with your constant whining. You need to shake it off, though. I'm telling you, it's not a good look. You're too dramatic. You need to let go of all that feminine, 'woe be to me', 'she was the only one' kind of thinking. That stuff is what keeps you in the gutter. So she dumped your ass and promptly shagged someone else. What's the big deal? Did you think she was going to turn to the lord and become a born-again virgin? Don't be an idiot. Who cares what she's doing? You need to focus on yourself, buddy. You need to be making moves, not dwelling on the moves others are making. It's the only thing that will make you feel better."

Mao generally recoiled from Ricardo's advice, but he knew the man was making sense. Mao nodded meekly. Ricardo sighed. As we mentioned, he was not accustomed to, and did not enjoy discussing feelings. 'Feelings', to Ricardo, were reserved for expressing how sore you felt after a big workout, or how much you enjoyed your last frivolous sexual encounter.

"Breakups are messy. I get it. I really do. God only knows I've been through more than my fair share of them. But listen, you can't let the thing consume you. You're a young man in your prime. Besides, you and I both know that girls these days just don't know what they want. You can't take them too seriously. On the one hand, they're force-fed all of this feminism poison, so that their brains think one way, and meanwhile their hormones pull them the other way. And there you are, caught in the eye of a hurricane, a shmuck just trying to fix something you didn't break. There's simply no winning. I mean, look at this. No, really, look!"

Ricardo pulled out his smartphone, and pulled up one of his social media feeds.

"Look! Look at it! Fake tits, fake asses, and tattoos. Always the same. Look! Tits, asses, tattoos."

Ricardo brought the phone up to his face, steadily raising his voice as he continued to scroll.

"Honey, baby, sweetie, what am I going to do with that dragon tattooed on your ass? The last time you were in the kitchen, you couldn't figure out how to boil water!"

Ricardo was working himself up again, and getting louder. Mao was doing his best to suppress his laughter, trying to keep it together. People at other tables were looking over at Ricardo, who was making every sort of hand gesture and jabbing at the screen with his index finger.

"Look at this!"

Ricardo suddenly locked the screen and put the phone away.

"Did your ex even cook for you, bro? Did she clean?"

Mao tried to answer but Ricardo cut him off.

"Of course she didn't! Yet you're the asshole for wanting a woman who can take care of you. It's only normal that we 'man up' and make more money than her, *and* we're not allowed to sleep with any other women, even if they're literally throwing themselves at us, *and* we have to, within a reasonable timeframe that is to her liking, provide her with a diamond ring that entitles her to half our shit should she ever frivolously decide that she's done with us. Oh! It's so *easy* for a man to work like a dog to prove himself worthy, and for him to pretend that sleeping with the same woman over, and over, and over again until he's memorized that pussy from every imaginable angle was all he ever wanted, denying every fiber of his being that screams for him to fill every hole he can like a bee pollinating a field. But for a woman to cook and clean for him meanwhile, to take the edge off a man's burdensome role in the whole charade, call the goddamn police! Arrest this scumbag for chauvinism, misogyny, sexism, and so forth! Bring him to the guillotine, and chop his dick off!"

Almost everyone was looking at Ricardo now. He had worked up a little sweat, and was dabbing his forehead with his napkin. Mao was embarrassed, but couldn't help laughing. The whole thing was so over the top.

Ricardo took a deep breath, and reached over to pat his friend on the shoulder.

"Look at me, Mao. I am what I am. I'm a man, I love sex, I love sex with almost everyone, and I make no goddamn apologies for either of those facts. If men were supposed to be stripped of their killer instinct, and softened into dependable, predictable, and feminized yes-men, then guess what? *I* would never get laid. By either gender. But guess what? You and I both know all about that."

Mao was still laughing.

"Okay, okay, relax Rick. I'm on your team. We're in public. You're making a scene."

Ricardo slammed his hands on the tabletop and screamed:

"You think I care what these people think? That's *exactly* your problem. You've got to stop caring what people think, and start worrying about what *you* think. You're a lion! Go out and eat some goddamn gazelles, or whatever the hell lions do. Stop being such a pansy about it! That's all that matters!"

Mao was seriously concerned they would get thrown out.

"Alright, alright, relax!"

Ricardo took another deep breath. All of a sudden, he was cheerful. The internal wiring had overheated, triggering a system reboot.

"Anyway, there's nothing to worry about!"

Ricardo smiled widely, as he reached over for Mao's napkin.

"I'm here for you buddy. No more drama, you understand? From now on, you're going to be like me, rock steady, like a man."

Ricardo pounded his chest with his fist, while he dabbed at his sweaty forehead with what used to be Mao's napkin.

"A man, got it? No more drama."

With that, Ricardo stood up.

"*Hey! Du service aujourd'hui? Tabarnac!*"

The din stopped, and a fork could be heard crashing against the floor as everyone stopped and looked at Ricardo.

He sat back down, satisfied.

The waitress promptly came over. She was flustered, but didn't seem to have noticed Rick's outburst, or the fact that he was abnormally sweaty for a man in an upscale bistro on a snowy winter's day.

"Oh my gosh, I'm so sorry. We're so busy today. I didn't mean to leave you waiting so long."

The waitress had a cute, functional French accent. Her blonde hair was pinned up with just a lock left loose, so that it kept falling over her eyes whenever she looked down at her pad and pen. Mao thought it was endearing.

The waitress was clearly having a tough day. Ricardo noticed this, and composed himself with remarkable speed. As a big fan of the novel *American Psycho,* Mao recognized this stark and almost inhuman transition as the hallmark of a psychopath. Ricardo put on a big, gentle smile, and did what he always did: he took control of the situation.

"Hey sweetheart, hey, it's alright. I was just being a little theatrical, trying to prove a point to my friend, here. He's having a bit of a hard time lately. We know you're doing your best, and we're glad you're finally here."

The girl smiled, as Ricardo leaned back and touched his index finger to his upper lip, appraising the beautiful girl standing before him.

"You know something? You look absolutely stunning today. Has anyone told you that? No, I can tell they haven't."

The girl blushed and almost lost her grip on the notepad.

"It's a damn shame, too, because you do. Doesn't she look gorgeous today, Mao?"

Mao smirked, and nodded in agreement.

"What's your name, sweetheart?"

"Joliane" she replied shyly.

"Ah, what a beautiful name. I'm Ricardo, Joliane, pleasure to meet you. Let me ask you something, Joliane. What time do you get off work? I can imagine you're looking forward to it."

Joliane's reaction almost made Mao sick. She twirled her hair and bit her lip.

"At four."

Ricardo smiled.

"At four. That's wonderful. Because at four o'clock, I'm going to be waiting for you outside in my car. You see it there? It's the midnight blue Maserati across the street. Yes, that one."

Joliane's eyes sparkled with curiosity as she took it all in.

"You and me are going to go out tonight and have a little fun. I think it'll be good for you after a tough day. What do you say?"

Joliane looked around, making sure her boss wasn't watching. Then she straightened her skirt, and assumed a professional tone.

"Okay. Sure. That sounds good Ricardo."

She flashed her pretty, confident smile.

"Great. As for right now, we're going to make it easy on you. You'll bring me and my friend here two *Pince* burgers and two

Stella's, along with the bill right away, so that we can get out of your hair. How's that sound to you, Joliane?"

The waitress scribbled the order on her pad.

"Two *Pince* burgers and two Stella's. Coming right up."

Joliane winked and walked off, with both men watching the sway of her hips: one with hopeless longing, and the other with eager anticipation.

"You know, no matter how many times I see you do that, I never cease to be amazed."

Ricardo smiled across the table at Mao.

"The brain cannot override the body my friend. You just need to project confidence. It's a woman's intuition. They can tell if it's real or not. See, that's the problem with your prince, babe. He spends too much time thinking, and not enough time doing. He needs to find himself a Ricardo to set him straight."

Mao laughed.

"Rick, you ever hear of the term 'toxic masculinity'?"

Both men were grinning.

"I tell you what, Mao. Tonight, I'm going to run a social experiment for you. I'm going to shag that pretty little thing up, down, and sideways until she's speaking in tongues, channeling the Holy Spirit. If at any point the words 'toxic masculinity' come through, I'll be sure to let you know."

Oh, how the two of them laughed.

After lunch, Ricardo dropped Mao off near his car. The two men said a quick goodbye and parted ways.

Mao walked up a snowy Boulevard Saint Laurent, watching the people passing him by without so much as a second look. When he finally got in his car, he started it, then pulled out his smartphone. In his 'Notes' application, he wrote:

The heart wants what the heart wants. The brain, on the other hand, must find a way to accept that the wanting will never end.

He was satisfied with the realization, and with its expression. Ricardo was right. She was just some girl. She was just some girl. She was just some girl, until she broke his heart.

He pulled out his smartphone again, and wrote:

To try and right the wrong, is in itself wrong. There never was any wrong. Everything happens for a reason.

He liked that one. It made him smile.

So, he put the car in drive and went home.

XII

Fragments of Mao's Notes
20/12/2019

None of this matters. I'm just a fly on the wall. Well, no. I don't like 'fly on the wall'. I like impacting things. Agency. But, I don't know, there's something to that. The fly on the wall. Because when I'm writing, I use it. I look at things, and really try to accurately capture their essence in words.
Why is it important to disassociate from things?
Because then you can think more purely about the thing in question, without the thick lens of 'I' coloring what you see.

Some people go looking for reasons to carry on. Others go looking for reasons to quit.
And since you're the one making all the reasons, you always find what you're looking for.

HOW TO BE GREAT
Look at Bukowski. He's well-read, and he is prolific. He doesn't lay it on thick with the books and the academia, though. He lays it on thick with the Bukowski. That's what you want to do. Lay it on thick with the you, just as soon as you can figure who 'you' is.

The Cliché

For more information, please visit www.smallmindedplebeians.org
The donate button is located in the top right-hand corner of the
page.
Please give generously.

Love is just the vision of a better world.

XIII

A few short weeks after his bizarre encounter with the mysterious fuchsia-robed man in the building lobby, Mao was once again holed up in his twenty-first century isolation chamber (also known as an apartment). It was a cold, snowy Saturday afternoon, and Mao was doing what he always did on cold, snowy Saturday afternoons: he was reading. What was Mao reading? Why, that is an excellent, excellent question our most perceptive and inquisitive reader! As it turned out, Mao was reading *James and the Giant Peach* by the late, great Roald Dahl. Yes, a wonderful, classic book. But Mao wasn't twelve years old, was he? Reader, you are once again spot on! Mao was in fact not twelve years old. What Mao *was,* reader, was a twenty-seven-year-old man feeling blue. And why was he feeling blue? Well, for one, he was separated from the woman he loved. Or, thought he loved... and all that inevitable confusion. Then he was also struggling to overcome his writer's block in order to write the generational novel that would win him the fame, fortune, and adulation of millions that were his destiny. Poor old Mao was still brooding over all the blame his lost lover had laid at his feet (which, not so shockingly, was pretty much all of it), and blaming himself perhaps as fervently as she had for the way things ended. On top of it all, the unfortunate bastard was racking his brains as to how his writer's block could possibly be persisting in spite of the fact that he, for months now, had been suffering rather acutely.

Not much was making any sense to our poor old Mao.

Though really, reader, you should have known all of that already. Compliments aside, we expect you to take things just a little more seriously from here on out.

Are you paying attention?

You're not just meant to read the lines, you know.

You're meant to read between them, too!

Mao was writing a little, at least. As we've seen, though, that writing was coming in fits and starts, and he was having a very hard time piecing any of it together into any sort of continuity. He couldn't work out how all these little fragments shooting out of him haphazardly could possibly fit together into a novel, or into a coherent narrative of any kind. And so, Mao was reading Roald Dahl's *James and the Giant Peach* for one simple reason: Roald Dahl's books were completely madcap and ridiculous. Reading Roald Dahl's madcap and ridiculous tales made Mao's own madcap and ridiculous tale, that is, life, feel just a little less absurd by comparison. And feeling even just a little less absurd always cheered Mao up.

However, that afternoon as Mao lay on his old, dubiously cushioned excuse for a couch trying his best to read, he kept getting distracted. It wasn't that he was failing to abstract himself from all the problems whizzing neurotically around his mind, or that the book he was reading was overly complicated. Neither was the reading material inspiring in him kaleidoscopic trains of thought dashing off in every direction faster than he could follow them (as, alas, was the case in his most creatively fertile moments). Instead, as you may have guessed by the passing mention of the fuchsia-robed man at the very beginning of the feature, Mao again had to deal with those pesky and ever-present sounds emanating from the apartment across the hall. And those sounds were even peskier and even stranger than usual on that snowy afternoon.

The noises had become something of a regular occurrence, ever since he had encountered the enigmatic fuchsia-robed man in the lobby (whose serpentine and singularly foreign name Mao could not, for the life of him, remember). But, Mao hadn't yet put two and two together. This is probably because Mao wasn't, all things considered, anywhere near as bright as he thought he was.

Altogether unlike you, brilliant and esteemed reader!

At any rate, Mao was getting quite sick of it. He wasn't one for unnecessary confrontation, although he wasn't one to shy away from it, either. Especially if he thought he was right. And Mao, like most mortals, usually did think he was right.

He just couldn't *live* this way. He couldn't fully immerse himself in James' ridiculous *adventure* with that constant racket coming from across the *hall*. It wasn't at all your typical apartment complex creaks, bumps and knocks. Mao knew that people were generally brutes, and that noisiness was to be expected of brutes.

But these! These were sounds of another sort! These were guttural *declarations*! These were primordial *admonitions*! These were supernatural *incantations* that seemed to be summoned from another dimension!

Mao had just arrived at the passage in *James and the Giant Peach* when the crazy old man comes out of the bushes to give little boy James an unmarked paper bag filled with thousands of small, dry, magic 'crocodile tongues', which James later spills near his peach tree to spawn the titular 'giant peach'. (We feel impelled to take a moment's pause to applaud the very, very interesting symbolism employed by Mr. Dahl. It all works together beautifully. In fact, the most unlikely thing about the book is not the giant, building-sized peach, or even the human-sized talking bugs living within it, but rather the idea that there would be a benevolent whackjob of an old man waiting in the bushes of Northern England for a vulnerable, solitary child to pass by, only to fulfill his transient role in the child's story by handing him some magic tongues, without so much as laying a hand on said vulnerable and completely solitary child, whom this whackjob waited for ever so patiently day and night, we might add, and in spite of the fact that said child might never even have shown up! All that faith and hard work to hand him a sack of 'magic tongues'. And then, no explanation whatsoever for why James was chosen as the recipient of this sack of tongues, or any hint of an origin or afterthought for the whackjob in the bushes. Never mentioned again in the rest of the story. But hey. That is the beauty of children's books. They are under no obligation *whatsoever* to resemble the real world in any way, or to make any sense at all!) Mao had had to re-read the same sentence over and over again, while the whackjob next door seemed to be reciting an unintelligible mantra. This monosyllabic utterance the whackjob repeated over, and over, and over again, with subtle increases in intensity and volume, building to a moment of madness and fervor when who knows what would happen! Mao envisioned him breaking through the living room wall like the Kool-Aid man and offering him some ayahuasca. Suddenly, there was a loud ringing, as if the bells of the Notre Dame Cathedral were chiming just next door. The noise startled Mao. So much so that in his surprise, he theatrically flung the book he was reading into the air, as he simultaneously fell off the couch and straight onto his plump bottom.

"Why, what could the source of these strange sounds be?"

Mao pondered aloud, perplexed as he was perturbed. The book, drawn back to the earth by Newton's law of universal gravitation, landed on Mao's head, conveniently split at the very page that Mao was doggedly trying to read.

"My, my!" Mao mused, open book resting on head, "I suppose I'll just have to go next door and see. Mao will get to the bottom of this yet! Oh, yes indeed!"

With that, Mao leapt to his feet. He removed the book from its resting position on his cranium and placed a bookmark at the appropriate page. Then he placed the book down with care, opened his heavy chain-locked front door, and stomped indignantly across the checkered tiles and yellowing walls of the hall to the source of the disturbance: Apartment #8.

Why, reader, if only you could see how mightily flustered Mao was! Though, it must be said, beneath the frustration, Mao was also exceedingly curious.

Knock, knock, knock.

Mao pounded upon the door across the checkered tiles and yellowing walls of the hall.

Knock, knock, knock.

He pounded still, muttering all the while: "Can you believe the gall?"

Beyond the heavy door that led out into the hall, the strange chimes and guttural emanations suddenly stopped. Mao's impression was that the person inside might have been startled by the unexpected knock, and he heard the figure within shuffling about, doing its best, one would presume, to get his or her or they or them's things in order before coming to the door to courteously greet the unexpected, but never unwelcome company. When the shuffling stopped, Mao could hear the strange entity within tiptoeing ever-so-gently to the door. *To take a peek through the peephole,* Mao deduced.

One can never be too careful when there's an unexpected knock at the door!

On the other side of door #8, Jajùmissu Cá, it shall be duly stated, was in the middle of a rather busy work week, and was a little put off by the sudden interruption of his very important work. He was smack in the middle of filming his very first video séance with the dead (for his budding YouTube channel @Mysticofmimijad, seventy thousand subscribers and growing) when the loud and persistent knocking ruined his signoff. He walked softly to the door, his bare caramel feet and flowing robes hardly making a sound, and stole a glance through the peephole. With his eye up to the peephole, J.C. peeped Mao's frowny face and black piggy eyes staring back at him.

'Ah, it is the lovely young man from the lobby. What could he possibly be so grumpy about?' J.C. wondered. 'Perhaps the time has come for *The Mystic of Mimijad* to finally be of service!' He rubbed his hands together agreeably. He had taken up the habit of referring to himself regally in the third person. Aside from helping him stay in character, the eccentricity also bolstered his credibility with both potential clients and YouTube subscribers.

The mystic reached for the handle and opened the door quickly, announcing himself with a flourish of swaying robes and a lifted chin. At the sight of J.C., Mao's bushy eyebrows ascended high up above his flustered piggy eyes. Jajùmissu Cá, the man behind door #8, was still wearing the customary regalia of his homeland. He donned a floppy, white linen hat – one the likes of which Mao had never seen. J.C. wore long, thick necklaces of large black-or-white beads around his neck, which he fingered intently with his left hand as he peered across the threshold. In his other hand, he held a long, elegant Malacca cane, black as night, and with a golden handle in the shape of a jackal's head.

Through the open door, Mao's nose took in the full bouquet of scents escaping into the hall from within. Firstly, J.C. himself smelled oddly sterile, as though he had just been released from hospital care, or from prolonged captivity in a septic tank. From the interior of the apartment behind him trailed the scents of eucalyptus, probably from the incense burning within, and the faint, though not unappetizing scent of recently made macaroni and cheese.

"Why, young man, it is lovely to see you! You have come to take me up on my offer?"

Jajùmissu Cá's sonorous voice filled the hall with warmth. He was affecting a British accent, which he felt added to his persona's air of mystique. Mao didn't notice, of course, because the accent Jajùmissu Cá was affecting sounded, to Mao's ears, at most three percent British. The other ninety-seven percent was still the dominant strand of mangled cereal box English Mao heard every time J.C. opened his mouth.

"Your offer?"

Mao was so taken by the regalia, the smells, and the towering man responsible for the display that he had forgotten why he had even ventured across the hall. Jajùmissu Cá didn't bat an eye, of course. By then, he was used to this kind of dumbstruck reaction to his person. It seemed that Canadians couldn't quite figure out what to make of him. He saw the people staring at his sandals when he walked out of the snow and into the grocery store, or the pharmacy, or wherever, with his toes red and on the verge of frostbite.

"Indeed! Please, do, do come in!"

The invitation was grandiose. J.C. opened his arms wide in welcome, bowing and turning to the side. As the towering figure backed out of the way, Mao's inquisitive eyes hungrily scanned the interior of the most peculiar apartment.

Despite the fact that it was small, the apartment had, how should we say?

J.C.'s apartment had a very big personality.

Though the man himself looked neat and orderly, the apartment he lived in was in utter disarray. Then again, it struck Mao as a sort of deliberate disarray, a controlled chaos that emanated a certain kitschy, carnivalesque charm. Something the Japanese might call *wabi sabi*. Let us try and capture the essence of what Mao saw:

The center of the main room just beyond the open door was left mostly bare. Although, Mao quickly realized, the perimeter of the space was chock-full of the strangest oddities and mystical paraphernalia Mao had ever seen. On the floor, rugs of varying sizes, colors, and textures were thrown about haphazardly, overlapping one another, and covering every inch of visible floor space. Some of these mismatched rugs were cleaner than others, though the cleaner ones were by no means given any preferential treatment with regards to their position in the layout. Neither were the ones with fewer tears in them. To the left of the room and hugging the wall was an old oak chest that looked like the kind one might find abandoned on a street corner, or perhaps being ludicrously upsold by a conniving capitalist running a 'thrift' store. Upon it rested a few small-to-medium-sized ceramic idols, hand-carved into primitive impressions of elephants and horses. These sat upon an old, authentic-looking wooden Ouija board, and beside it lay a starkly contrasting plastic skull. There was also a small box bursting with crystals, and also a box of polished animal teeth of varying sizes and colors. About a dozen candles were scattered about on top of the chest, and yet dozens more were scattered about on the floor. And every single wick, to Mao's horror, was lit. Mao watched the melting wax slowly dripping onto the top of the chest, or in some cases, directly onto the rugs.

Beside the chest was a frayed and beaten up velvet chesterfield in a once bright, but now fading crimson. In the back of the room, Mao caught sight of what looked to him like a plate of sliced onions, peppers, and lemons, with four teacup candles resting upon them in perfect rhombus formation. These candles, too, were lit, and dripping wax onto the vegetables and fruit below. However, for the sake of clarity, although he was intrigued by what this symbol could possibly represent, and to what rich cultural tradition it owed its origin, Mao couldn't be sure that the mysterious plate was actually topped with sliced onions, peppers, and lemons, because the plate was at the other end of the room, the room was dim but for the candle light, and though it looked like it was *clearly* a plate of sliced onions, peppers, and lemons with four lit teacup candles dripping wax onto the vegetables and fruit below in perfect rhombus formation, it also couldn't be, because that didn't make any sense. There were old plastic water bottles with the labels ripped off all over the place, and these were filled with what looked like a dark, syrupy liquid. Along the right wall, there was a TV monitor turned on, though half falling over on its stand and leaning against black curtains blocking any natural light from entering the room. The tilted screen was projecting those anachronistic black, white, and multicolor bars that, way back in the 1990's signaled 'no reception' or 'technical difficulties', but in 2019 signaled 'scene of heinous premeditated crime'. Beneath the monitor, there lay a large, smooth, white plastic surface where seven small polished shells were neatly bunched beside a sinister-looking gothic candelabra, a plush conch shell full to the brim with five, ten, and twenty-dollar bills, a taxidermy squirrel that was holding... yes, it was holding a large, ornately cast silver cross, and finally, a large ceramic bowl overflowing with earthy, unwashed beetroot.

Amidst all the burning candles and near the center of the room, a smartphone was sitting atop a tripod pointed directly at the red velvet chesterfield.

Jajùmissu Cá kept bowing the entire time that Mao stood there savoring the strange sights and smells of this most perplexing Apartment #8, just across the checkered tiles and yellowing walls of the hall connecting it to Mao's Apartment #7. As the magic (or madness) wore off, Mao remembered the reason he had ventured across the hall in the first place. He shook himself out of the trance.

"What in God's good name were you doing in there?"

J.C. stood up straight. He was beaming.

"Oh, miboy, I was making the most jolly-good video for my YouTube channel. Have you heard of the YouTube, young man?"

Mao looked his kooky neighbor up and down, but took it in stride. He smacked his lips and nodded coolly.

"YouTube? I may have heard of it."

Jajùmissu Cá chuckled wholeheartedly.

"Of course, of course you know of the YouTube! It is one of the great inventions of your generation, miboy! Infinite content always at your fingertips! I was performing a video séance with the dead, you see. That is why I was making maybe a bit much noise!

I called up the ghost of Elvis for my subscribers, young man. You know Elvis, miboy? Yes, yes! Elvis is always one of the more chatty ghosts. He loves to talk about his death. You know, Dr. Nick and the twelve thousand pills he prescribed. I got him to clear the air. Mystery solved! Next week we do John F. Kennedy."

Jajùmissu Cá was smiling ear to ear. Mao had absolutely no idea what he was talking about. J.C. leaned in and whispered:

"Mr. Elvis said he is finding it very hard to find qaaludes in the afterlife."

Jajùmissu Cá flashed a toothy grin that revealed his satisfaction with the witticism. Mao, on the other hand, wasn't sure what was happening. He felt like he was being laughed at, but that couldn't be. This man was clearly the joke. Mao blinked three times, but Jajùmissu Cá was still there. He frowned and thought for a second. Yes, yes. He was sure he hadn't uttered the word 'Beetlejuice' even once today.

Jajùmissu Cá adjusted his floppy hat. His face was suddenly solemn.

"You must to come in and chat with me, miboy. I can tell from just a look at you that you have troubles, young man. Grave troubles. But lucky for you, I can help."

Mao's skepticism was right out there on his sleeve.

"Right. Look," Mao sighed, "what was your name again?"

Jajùmissu Cá smiled his toothy smile.

"Jajùmissu Cá, miboy. But my subscribers and patients know me as the Mystic of Mimijad."

'What a *whackjob*', Mao thought.

"Mhm. I see. The Mystic of Jajumijad, got it. Look, I'm next door trying to read, and your bells and animal noises are really distracting. Also, those candles look like a fire hazard. You think you can cut it out?"

Jajùmissu Cá was not expecting this. He raised an eyebrow of his own. The boy had his walls firmly up... he would prove a tough nut to crack.

"Ah, reading is very good for the mind, as for the soul. It must be quite the important, challenging book that you are tackling, for you to have come all the way across the hall to ask for quiet. If I may, what is this important, compelling book that you are studying today, young man?"

Mao blushed. He wasn't about to admit his righteous indignation was motivated by struggling to read a children's book. He wasn't about to let himself be judged! Not by this lunatic!

"It doesn't matter what I'm reading, it's... none of your business, okay? Just tone it down. No more stomach ache or dying animal noises. *Capisce*?"

J.C. narrowed his eyes.

"Yes, of course. I am done for the day, anyhow."

J.C.'s eyes darted around, and the tone of his voice became suddenly ominous, and prophetic.

"Young man, I can see that you are not a believer. But I can see also that you are intrigued by the Mystic of Mimijad, and impressed by his atelier. I know there is something. Something inside. I know there is someone, or something that is haunting you. Yes. You stink of a soul harboring ghosts. You radiate the aura of the unresolved. It will eat you from within, miboy. Like a parasite. I guarantee it. Yes. There is something deep inside of you, eating you from the inside. It is yearning to come out, isn't it?"

The manic change in the big man's demeanor sent a chill down Mao's spine. The mystic's eyes widened, and as he pointed his black Malacca cane at Mao, his voice became swollen with intensity.

"Yes, you see! I know you see! Be not afraid, miboy. I will reach in, and I will help you pull it out. I will help you face your demons, and vanquish them! I will set you free, and make you whole again!"

Jajùmissu Cá took a deep breath, as he threw back his head and looked down his nose at Mao. Mao, who envisioned the skies parting and lightning summoned by the Mystic of Mimijad's villainous magic raining down, began to shake just ever so slightly. J.C. narrowed his eyes as he exhaled, then brought his bright eyes level with Mao's. The mystic spoke with an icy calm.

"But there is no rush. You will come to me... when the time is right."

Mao stood there staring, slack jawed and terrified, calculating whether J.C. was guru, god... or circling back to gag.

After what seemed an eternity, Mao once again regained control over his heart rate.

"Okay. I'll let you know when I'm ready. For now, me and my demons are on working terms. Please, just try to keep it down, alright? Have a good evening, Mr. Mimijad."

"My name is Jajùmissu Cá!" The powerful voice boomed.

Then, all at once, it was sweet:

"Mimijad is my homeland. You may refer to me as the Mystic of Mimijad, if you wish, or simply as J.C."

The walking stick was transferred to the left, as the open palm of the right was extended. Mao stared at the hand before reaching out hesitantly to shake it. But as his fingers touched J.C's, he was jolted by an electric shock.

"Ouch!"

Mao yanked his hand away, and rubbed it. It was those blasted rugs! The mystic laughed deviously as he cupped his hands around the golden jackal and leaned on his Malacca cane.

"Nice to officially meet you, Jaju... J.C. My name is Mao."

'Mao? Is this white boy messing with me?' J.C. wondered. Yet, as the consummate professional he was, he would not let anything undermine his poise, no matter how farfetched or outlandish. In his line of work, of course, acknowledging *anything* as preposterous would be instant career suicide.

"Pleasure to meet you, though I already knew your name was Mao. I felt it when we met in the lobby. It was written that you and I would cross paths, miboy. I look forward to seeing you again soon."

With that, J.C. bowed, and receded into the shadows of his apartment as the door swung swiftly shut.

Mao returned uneasily to his apartment. He closed the door behind him and picked up his copy of *James and the Giant Peach*.

'Gosh, what a strange fellow that is who lives next door', he thought to himself, as he settled onto the couch and picked up where he left off, reading on about the giant Centipede's obsession with his boots.

XIV

Alright, so maybe we were a little hard on the Arctic Monkeys' 2013 album *AM*. We mean, we're coming around to it. We guess it never resonated before. We guess we never understood that... 'poetic pretty boy' aesthetic, or that 'my heart aches but I'm making due with my million interim lovers' kind of headspace before. Then again, spending all this time watching over Mao probably had something to do with our change of heart. Or, we don't know. Maybe we simply didn't like the fact that Alex Turner was out there proving that bravado in the face of heartache wasn't an original sentiment. And maybe we were just slightly jealous that he could pull it off better than we could.

Not that the incorporeal care all that much about sex appeal...

Frankly, it's an absolute mystery to us how any organism burdened with hormones and reproductive organs could ever manage to get anything useful done at all.

Maybe it's just that *AM* is a breakup album, and again, as incorporeal, we can't much relate. Besides, so much of that pop rock breakup scene is just a bunch of noise pollution, you know? Like, oh, look out, he's obviously just sad, but he's going to try to fool you, and more importantly himself with a new haircut and a leather jacket!

It seems so cliché.

So... overdone.

Another thing is that as a timeless, discarnate narrator, we could never seem to find a leather jacket that fit right.

Our shoulders aren't broad enough.

Or, our shoulders aren't existent enough to be broad enough.

Yeah, we suppose that after watching Mao for the last little while, we can relate a tad more. It occurred to us that maybe the defiance, though *obviously* transparent, is necessary. Maybe the transparency is the point. Maybe the vulnerability needs to be processed slowly, and the leather jacket helps to take one's mind off of things in the interim, when one's tendency might be to maybe stay in one's lane, and to avoid ruffling any feathers. Maybe there is something to all that 'fake it 'til you make it' propaganda everyone is always harping on about.

Let's be clear: *AM* is a highly danceable album. And we've been told it's easy to drink to. The women folk really seem to like it, and that's always a plus (for organisms with reproductive organs, anyway).

Another thing that we think is cool about *AM* is its neat ending. Alex Turner performed a magic trick with the last song on the album, titled 'I Wanna Be Yours'. The song was, in fact, originally a poem written by British punk-poet John Cooper Clarke, who was an early and enduring influence on Alex Turner's world-renowned lyricism. Which is so interesting to us, because a fan of the band would hardly realize the words of 'I Wanna Be Yours' weren't Alex Turner's own, without first doing a little digging. It is remarkable the way he sings the song so emotively, and the lyrics seem so in line with the rest of his body of work, and so plausibly his own.

Furthermore, the poem that inspired the song was popular in its own right, and was apparently used (and probably still is) by a whole lot of saps in England to propose to their ladies. That British sense of humor, you gotta love it! The poem/song includes some interesting subject matter, such as the way that the speaker pathologizes his love for the object of his desire to the point of comparing himself to consumer products like a vacuum cleaner or a Ford Cortina, which he hopes his love interest will make use of in order to make her life that much easier and more convenient. Talk about self-effacing devotion! *Honey, we decided that we love you so much, we're going to have ourselves genetically redesigned into a car for you, so you can drive us to work every day! No, really, we don't mind! It's not like we have anything better going on in our miserable lives! You are our only reason to be alive. And we love having your ass in our face first thing in the morning!*

However, the most interesting thing about *AM*'s closing song is the intertextuality of the piece, and the way that it comments on what art really is, you know? Like, art is just this big amorphous blob of works and pieces and projects that every artist is not only able to, but is supposed to get their hands on, and play with, and rework into something new that they can call a contribution, thus expanding the canon of contributions and works and pieces and projects that is <u>ART</u>.

You dig?

Alex Turner loved John Cooper Clarke's work so much that he paid homage to it by making it his own. Thus, 'I Wanna Be Yours' expands and grows, as does John Cooper Clarke, as does *AM*, as does rock n' roll, as does music, and so on, and so forth.

We don't know. Maybe we're making a lot out of nothing. The album has a lot going for it. We think it will certainly go down as the breakup album of the millennium. And that's saying a lot, because as of 2019, there are still over nine hundred years to go in this one. For mortals, anyway.

Mao's favorite song on the album was always 'No.1 Party Anthem'. Do yourself a favor, and look the lyrics up if you have a minute.

XV

So it's the year 2015 and a twenty-two-year-old Mao is on the prowl, wondering whether she left already or not. It's early September, so he's got a leather jacket on – brown I-can't-believe-it's-not-leather, actually – and he looks really good, all things considered.

He's in some dingy pub up a flight of dilapidated stairs somewhere on Crescent Street, and the last he saw of her, she was smiling flirtatiously over her cocktail as he leaned over the bar and sucked nonchalantly on his beer. This is the fourth pub they've been to on this crawl, tuition-funded, we might add, a group of thirty or so undergraduates. Idiots, of course, the lot of them are, but blissfully ignorant of the fact. Ah, to be twenty-two, and not yet responsible for oneself. To be forgiven so much, to have all the rights of a fully-grown adult, and simultaneously the widest possible breadth of fuck-up leeway one will ever possess. It's enough to make you feel like you've been sprinkled in pixie dust that immunizes against responsibility, and its inevitable successor, misery.

There's some party anthem or other on, encouraging the kids to *always* buy more beer, or to do some other incredibly stupid thing that would compromise their longevity, and so naturally also raise their social status among the other twenty-somethings sprinkled in that very same pixie dust.

As he exits the washroom, hair in order, and *what hair he had*, confidence brimming and witty opener in tow, Mao struggles for a second to remember her name. Her name. Oh, for fuck's sake, what was it? It was something mythical. Persephone? Fitting, for that would make him Hades, but no. It wasn't quite that exotic. Penelope? Yes, that was it. Sweet and sexy Penelope. No doubt she'd be waiting faithfully by the bar while he made his odyssey to the pisser.

He walks past the ceramic clacks and the frayed felt of the pool tables, dodging the spilt beer and drunken cackling jocks wearing sunglasses indoors (par for the course), without breaking stride, strutting along like only a cocksure twenty-two-year-old with a leather jacket and a half-a-hard-on can, always maintaining that squinting look of detached appraisal he lifted from the oversexed rock n' roll videos he likes to watch, scanning the length of the bar for the blonde hair and the black denim that carefully hug those elegant, pear-shaped curves.

It was as you'd expect: tatty lights in the floor, sweat on the walls, and a motel next door with time-and-fluid-hardened sheets. All that was missing were the cages and poles, but there *was* a place around the corner... (there was always a place like that around the corner in Montréal). It was a perfectly set stage, where one could happily indulge in the charms of unobservant youth long before they turned stale, sad, and pathetic.

Indeed, it looked to be playing that way. Penelope had been rather forthright from the jump, but there was just a small, tiny little hitch. Mao had a girlfriend, and her name wasn't Penelope. For clarity's sake, it wasn't A–Z either.

We know, we know.

'Hrruumph, men are all the same!', you might be thinking, with a sour grimace on your face, if you usually seek a seated position before urinating. 'Ha! Men are all the same!', you might be thinking, with a grin, if you are a pig.

The truth was, Mao had called off the search for his soul a long while ago, or, at least, he meant to put it on hold again. He had a girlfriend, yes, but he meant to leave her. He had meant to leave her for a while, really. It wasn't that she even did anything wrong. The girl loved him. She treated him very well. He just didn't see himself marrying her. She was sweet, and he loved her, but he just wasn't *in love* with her.

Besides, he was too young for all that.

He shouldn't have been speaking to Penelope to begin with, but how could he resist the reckless confidence she exuded? In the first of the series of dingy holes on the crawl, he saw her leaning against the wall, having a sly indoor smoke. She was talking to some guy. He was over six feet tall, *obviously*. Ladies, let's just get one thing clear: just because he can reach the top shelf, doesn't mean he can *reach the top shelf.* And she was telling some wacky tale about how the folks who ran this place were her oldest friends. No, that's too much, she wasn't. She was actually telling some improbable anecdote about how her subnormal father broke his leg riding a Harley Davidson into one of those huge, antiquated satellite dishes that jut out of the ground like intergalactic homing beacons.

This is where Mao made his move.

Between sips of his drink, he laughed loudly at the story's conclusion. The elongated ape, on the other hand, ruined his chances by standing there and taking what was no doubt the most absurd thing he'd ever heard in his life at face value. Penelope, who was a frolicking bundle of sexual energy, naturally gravitated toward the more lighthearted of her options. They locked eyes, and all the signals were sent. She smiled, and her nose ring gleamed in the murky light, while her eyes invited him to approach.

So, he did.

From that moment on, she had laughed at nearly everything he said, like the voices in her head were constantly telling her imaginary jokes only she could hear. It wasn't even that Mao wasn't funny, the kid was doing well, it's just that no one is *that* funny, unless you *really* want to fuck them. (Ah, those notorious reproductive organs!). Mao, for his part, tried and tried to swallow those lumps in his throat that were made partly of nervousness and guilt, and partly of the excitement inspired by the prospect of forbidden fruit.

It should be stated: she *did* look good.

She had dirty blonde hair and rouged lips. She had an experienced, salacious arch to her lips when she smiled. She wore a tight, white, long-sleeved top with a very deep v, and the black high-rise denim. Both the pants and the shirt were amply full.

One might say she was a certified mind-blower.

Like many women, she liked to talk. After suggesting there was somewhere from which he might know her, just to get the ball to roll, she went on a drunken monologue about her perverted roommate, who often exposed himself to her, and about how she didn't mind so much, because he was kinda hot, and also he let her live in his apartment rent-free. She told Mao about her ex-boyfriend, whose parents came from the same small village in Northern Quebec as hers did, about her suspicions that they might have been distantly related, but ultimately about how he was an inadequate lover she was glad to be rid of. She told Mao about how she almost started a fire the other day, forgetting the frozen pizza she threw in the oven before hitting her bong and running a bath. Mao kept his eyes in a squint, sucked on his beer, nodded, and when appropriate, concurred with whatever whimsical sentiment the beautiful mental patient expressed. She told him about her journalistic aspirations, as she coolly pulled a vial from her pocket and downed what she explained was the last of her penicillin, with a big swig of her sour drink. Mao didn't ask, Penelope didn't tell. It was none of his business, really. And good for her for keeping such a close eye on her health.

After what seemed like an eternity, but was really only about a half hour of her yapping, Mao was feeling a little confused, because it wasn't like he was going to fall in love with this strumpet...

He just wanted her to do him no good, and really, she looked like she could!

That was when he left for the bathroom. He was on his fifth, or maybe sixth pint after all, and he had yet to break the seal. Rounding the pool tables, he noticed the blonde hair cascading down the back of her head. She turned, drink in hand, and the straw resting gently between those plump, smiling red lips. It was the look of love, alright, and Mao felt the ensuing rush of blood! He smiled back, but suddenly, there was a feeling something like indigestion in the pit of his stomach. Something wasn't sitting right, and it wasn't the dubious nachos from two pubs prior.

It was the dubious morality of everything that had happened *since* the nachos.

And then it all hit him, walloped him really. A wave of good sense burst through the veneer of beer-induced stupor, and slapped him right across the face. Who did he think he was? He couldn't go through with this. This just wasn't the way he did things. His views on God were up in the air, but he definitely believed in some sort of 'what goes around comes around' cosmic order. Was he really going to screw his future self over for a quick screw?

As he approached the beautiful girl, with his bladder emptied and his scruples replenished, he felt his immediate desire pitted against his future and his values. Would he be the man who threw everything out the window for carnal pleasure, or would he be the man of character he always wanted to see when he looked in the mirror?

He put his arm around her.

"Penelope, this has been a lot of fun, but..."

She affected her own seductive squint, as she gently pressed her forefinger to his lips. She leaned in and whispered into his ear, while artfully nibbling at his earlobe:

"There is something I need to tell you."

That rush of blood, it's enough to singlehandedly recondition a man's view of the world...

She leaned back slowly, keeping her lowered eyes firmly on his. Still smiling that devious smile, she pulled a tube of crimson lipstick from her purse. She took hold of his forearm, pulled his sleeve up, and uncapped the lipstick with her teeth. Mind you, her eyes never left his. She looked down, and wrote on his forearm in the red wax. Done, she touched herself up, and put the lipstick away. She leaned in again, bit his earlobe harder, and whispered:

"Let me know what you think."

Mao raised an eyebrow, and looked down at his forearm. There, he saw the blood red calling of the she-devil.

It read simply: 'I want to fuck you.'

His lips involuntarily parted and his heart rate quickened, as every single drop of available blood was frantically pumped to the swollen scene of the crime, and his semi evolved to its final form. He looked into her eyes, and she smiled and winked at him.

"Excuse me, I, uh, I... I'll be right back," he sputtered.

And with that, he turned, and walked briskly down the stairs of the dingy pub, while the party anthem blasting out of the speakers bled imperceptibly into the next.

He hailed a cab as he did his best to pack up his tent.

He never saw Penelope again.

Reader, when you fall from grace, you fall hard.

However, when you manage to tiptoe around the precipice, you might just get a good story out of it!

XVI

Excerpt from Mao's Journal
22/12/2019
Religion and Science –
WHAT DO I BELIEVE?

I've read a bit of Dawkins, and the arguments he makes against God and religion are compelling...to the rational mind. However, as many sages and bards have noted, existence is far from a purely rational endeavor.

As a storyteller, I find it difficult to accept the premise that there is no God. Here is why: just as I write, creating worlds as well as the characters that inhabit them, could I not also, by logical extension, be the simple hero of some grand, cosmic tale, which God alone could author? Or, perhaps, on days when I am feeling less sure of myself, couldn't I be a secondary character meant to populate the horizons of this yet-unmasked cosmic hero's world?

The canonical Judeo-Christian characterizations of God are silly, of course, and were obviously made up by humans. But that isn't the point, is it? Something still irks me. It is a fact that the earliest peoples to create or discover languages as communicative tools almost universally used those languages to express certain primordial truths they felt important, in spite of the fact that they *may not have fully understood them. This expression took the form of stories and myths. And so, wouldn't this fact confirm storytelling's intrinsic role in the evolution of human understanding? Then, there's also the curious fact that so many of these early myths, or the ones that somehow managed to survive throughout the ages and make it to me, anyway, refer to some grand, all-knowing, or all-powerful entity who created the world we mortals roam. Wouldn't that fact demonstrate the notion that the beyond, the unknowable, or 'God' has perhaps always been the single most powerful beacon guiding human thought? And then, what to make of the problem of humankind interpreting the unknown through stories? Well, what would our most primitive interpretations of the unknown be, if not attempts to convey a concept we could not then, and as of yet still cannot fully grasp? Could God be the original metaphor for human purpose? It seems plausible. In that way, that is, the way of human mythmaking and storytelling with the aim of making sense, metaphorically, of the vast and boundless realm beyond reason, isn't all of human history, all of existence just a story each and every one of us contributes to? Or, to use a clearer metaphor, couldn't life be just a text with countless authors?*

Modern, or rather, postmodern scholars agree that there is nothing outside the text – that humanity has created everything, including its own interpretations of self, nature, and God. But what inspired the interpretations? How to explain humankind's millennia of obsession with God?

It is all a little overwhelming, and I am not quite sure what to make of it, yet.

Overall, I think I am nestled somewhere between science and postmodern theory, and also somewhere between reason and God. I believe in objective reality, there is no question. Or, at least, I believe that the frequency or dimension shared by humans in consciousness is as close to an objective reality as any of us needs. But I cannot quite bring myself to subscribe to Dawkins' total faith in science. This is because I don't believe that a) science could ever entirely describe objective reality, or b) that the comprehensive description of objective reality would in any way unlock the mystery of its meaning. Certainly, science has served humanity greatly thus far (though I must bitterly acknowledge that it has come with its drawbacks), but I view science as an uncovering, or, better put, as the discovery and eventual opening of a door. Every door that science opens moves humanity forward into greater understanding and potential. However, every door that science opens also leaves humanity vulnerable to greater, and more complex snares. To continue the door metaphor, science leads into a room with countless other doors, where each of those doors open into rooms of their own, with countless other doors concealing countless other mysteries. You can see how this metaphor plays itself out. Both the universe and the human brain expand infinitely outward and infinitely inward, and so the very acceptance of the mathematical concept of 'the infinite', which also represents the full circle, the collapsing of binaries, convergence, perfection, and, consequently, transcendence, implies, for me, an acceptance of the incalculable nature of the 'beyond', and the inexhaustible nature of the grand mystery. Thus, in spite of the fact that most would never admit it, even mathematicians implicitly accept the idea of God as an axiom, though it is also their lifelong pursuit to find a way to put Him/It into a formula they can manipulate.

Acknowledgement of a higher power, or an underlying divine nature as an axiom of human existence, I think, is a concession to vulnerability, because it is a concession to the fact that there will always be something beyond our comprehension as human beings. For some, it may be difficult to accept the fact that we're not meant to know or control everything.

Ah, reader! To be able to let go, to be able to surrender to the sublime without the need for that pesky illusion of control! *Que será, será!* What will be, will be.

Of course, this is no trouble to us. But then, we have the privilege of timelessness. Unquestionably, reckoning one's existence in time simply must be a mortal's most daunting obstacle to enlightenment. For poor old Mao, the discovery of submission as an axiom of existence was something of a novelty. He wasn't sure, yet, where he fit into the eternal balance. Although, at least he could take solace in the fact that he was slowly becoming aware of something more. These things never happen quickly, reader. One must have patience. One must remain at all times playful with the sprites of the spiritual realm. The individualized human ego is very resilient to dissolution. That is why for the unhappy, Mao was beginning to understand, submission would always prove a challenge.

XVII

One frosty, late December morning, Mao awoke, got out of bed, and shivered. He slipped on his warmest pair of slippers and the sweater he had thrown on the floor near his bed the night before. With bloodshot eyes and in his tattiest pair of boxers, he looked a hot, mangled mess. His beard, which he had not shaved even once in the *months* since his breakup with A–Z, was tangled and unkempt, in keeping with the aura of tortured genius (insanity) he had been so carefully cultivating. And the reason his eyes were bloodshot? That was simple: he had consumed copious amounts of drink the night prior.

In his current condition, astute and perceptive reader, poor old Mao's future did not look promising. The drinking was indeed becoming a bit of a problem.

The worst part of it all, reader, was the reasoning behind the madness:

You see, Mao drank in an attempt to, much like Bukowski, whirl himself into a drunken stupor so potent it could offer him the necessary insight to cynically, but saliently rant against the shortcomings of society.

Self-destruction in the name of inspiration.

Did it work?

Our guinea pig was determined to find out.

But for the moment he was preoccupied with the fact that his mouth was dry and his body felt like an old, rusty wrench.

He walked over to the bathroom, groaning like the wounded beast he was, hoping to clear his head with an aspirin, to wash his face, and to drop the first magnificent and revitalizing deuce of the day.

About a half-hour later, he walked out of the lavatory feeling renewed, or at least, about a half-pound lighter. He proceeded to stumble to the kitchen, where he planned to make himself a grand, greasy, hangover-curing scrambled eggs and bacon breakfast. As he stumbled across the apartment with his head in the fluffy scrambled clouds, he noticed the door to his spare room was ajar.

'Hmm, I don't remember leaving that door open,' he thought.

Mao poked his head into the mostly empty room, and noticed his messy work desk, which he had been meaning to get back to for the longest, and the two bags of A–Z's things peering back at him. He rubbed his forehead and yawned.

"I've really got to get rid of that crap," he said aloud to no one in particular.

Then, he walked over to the fridge, without giving it a second thought.

\---

Have you ever thought, dear reader, of how a word's phonetics could impact the way it is interpreted? Or, whether the way a word *sounds* has anything to do with what it *means*? Take the word, *lingering*, for instance. The word makes us think of something elusive, like a shadow, a wisp of smoke, or even... a ghost. We all have ghosts *lingering* within us, don't we? Sometimes, we don't want to let them go, because the feeling of a phantom embrace is so comforting against the fear of the cold, harsh reality of true, undeniable solitude.

But then, ghosts haunt us for a reason, don't they?

As many a legend has told, the haunting usually arises from *unfinished business*. Perhaps this is why the hero of every story must venture into an underworld, of sorts. Yes, the descent into the shadows is an integral part of the hero's journey. In the darkness, reader, there is nowhere to hide, and no way to escape what lurks within. In the underworld, the hero must confront his ghosts, wrestle with the lesson they have to offer, and pay the dues that will finally set them to rest. Then, not only can the hero be set free, but the ghost can also be set free, finally able to complete its peaceful journey into the afterlife. In this way, and in this tried and tested way only, dear reader, can one be purged of a lingering ghost.

However, the first step to purging a ghost as to making a grand scrambled eggs and bacon breakfast, is to *want* to.

XVIII

The brain is an elusive organ, no doubt. Much of its work is done on inaccessible levels of the subconscious, in mysterious realms that manifest themselves and break through to the surface in the strangest, most puzzling ways.

As he slept, Mao's brain began to stir. He tossed and turned, grunted, and finally opened his eyes. It was the middle of the night, and the room was pitch black. He turned over on his side and reached for his handheld device on the nightstand. He unlocked the screen, and what he saw within shook him from his stupor.

He walked over to the picnic table.

She was already sitting, looking off into the distance.

She swung her head playfully to face him, the diamond in her nose glistening in the sunlight, her lips curved in a smile of recognition.

Mao's heart skipped a beat.

He sat there, static, lacerated by the vision of her beautiful, happy, smiling face.

It was really her.

Right there, across the table.

His heart swelled with the elation and pride of knowing that he had been the source of that graceful creature's happiness. That he had been the one to inspire that beautiful smile. He made to step forward, but then, the moment of ecstasy was never meant to last. It was necessarily followed by a moment of dissonance, the moment when he needed to realize that this was only a dream... and a treacherous one.

Though he wanted nothing more, he knew he could not touch her.

He was afraid it all would shatter.

He backed away, turned, and wandered aimlessly in a semi-conscious state, away from the table, away from the smiling face that marked the soft, warm center of his heart, the homing beacon of all his most intimate hopes and dreams. He resisted with all his might the breathless desperation slowly swelling to despair, as he walked the long, bright corridor of time, moving further and further away from her.

Until, he encountered the aqueous substance.

"Anything you like. Anything to get away," he cried out.

A sickly grin declared itself in an amorphous face accompanied by the slow nod of a fluid head. He followed close behind and was led to the red lights where the entity assumed a solid form: the Harlot, beckoning to her hollow. She sauntered in playfully, but Mao lost his nerve. Or, perhaps, found his resolve. He turned away once more, only to realize that he stood, *transfixed, on the lip of a bottomless pit. Looking behind him, he discovered suddenly that he was in an unfamiliar place, and there was no means of escape. He screamed out for help, a concentrated, piercing cry that was heard by no one.*

And then he fell.

It was a mere few seconds or eternities later that he mercifully awoke.

They say the subconscious speaks in symbols. And for what it's worth, we think 'they' got that one right. What is language itself, if not the grandest, most complex metaphor ever created?

As you already know, reader, the word 'bread' is not really bread. The word, and in fact all words, are merely the symbol, or proxy for the familiar sensory experience they evoke. The words 'bread', or 'hammer', or 'smartphone' point to the communal understanding of 'bread', 'hammer', and 'smartphone' that has arisen from each of their many distinct, though similar iterations in time. Most have experienced bread many times before, and have no trouble making the leap from the word 'bread' to the idea of bread. The same can be said for so many words for places, people, things, emotions, and experiences.

But how do these words, these symbols, work when ascribed to concepts that have no familiar sensory experience? How do we even begin to speak about the mysterious ingredients in the supernatural potion bubbling away in the grand cauldron of consciousness?

God? Purpose? Love?

What is the familiar sensory experience behind these proxies?

Can a word uttered or contemplated in time ever adequately symbolize a concept originating in the realm beyond time?

Do all words emanate from one single source, or are they all doomed to the distortion of individual fancies and whims?

Certainly good questions.

Without, as of yet, any certain answers.

It is difficult, in moments like the ones Mao experienced in the folds of his subconscious, to refute the inspiring properties of pain. Not having the thing you want most: it is an excellent means of reawakening the soul's most primal yearnings. Suffering: it is an excellent starting point for the contemplation of suffering, and by extension, of meaning.

It is the endeavor of channeling those primal yearnings and contemplations of suffering into something beautiful, cathartic, and meaningful that is, dear reader, the most highly indefinite of propositions. This is the artist's life's work. This is the artist's calling.

And all are called.

Though only few ever answer.

XIX

Excerpt from Mao's Journal
02/01/2020
The Creative Process as Self-Immolation –
HAPPY NEW YEAR

How can I create something new, something original, something good and worthwhile, if I'm the same old me every time I step forward to confront the abyss of the blank page, where what will be offered and swallowed has already been offered and swallowed a thousand times before? New Age practitioners say 'growth'. Spiritual practice and everlasting renewal. Buddhism, and the pursuit of Nirvana. In other words, self-immolation.

How do I create something new? I destroy one of the pillars holding up my sense of self, thus tilting the structure into a new structure, or better yet, demolishing it altogether. To rebuild something new out of the rubble, this is the noble practice of growth, of creating something new out of the old, something worthwhile from the no longer useful. To discover something inspiring in the dry springs of the past, to rise again like a phoenix from its ashes. To destroy myself, and then to rebuild, to placate the inner calling from the depths of my being that will never be satisfied with any sort of regularity or routine. Though, sometimes

I stop myself and ask: where is the nobility in this? Where is the nobility in robotically heeding to a call that one has no power to resist?

Repetition is boring. New, new, new. Destroy, destroy, destroy. Rebuild, rebuild, rebuild. But what if the dust of the pillars I've smashed becomes so fine, I can no longer remake of it anything solid? What if I don't know how to rebuild? And what if I smash the wrong pillar? Is there such an instance? Is there any pillar so foundational, that to destroy it would mean the end? Could I destroy the self so entirely that there is no rebuilding? Is that the ideal? To be shattered to the point of true and utter indifference? Is that bliss? Is that Nirvana? To be, like a vampire, one who looks into the mirror and sees naught?

No, not like a vampire, because self-immolation is selfless and noble, when it is done for a cause.

My cause is the artistic ideal. My cause is catharsis, for myself and for others. It is noble for me to lay myself down at the altar of the artistic ideal, casting aside all material pursuits and pleasures, in exchange for the fleeting chance at a most unlikely dance with a beauty whose lips bear the taste of the everlasting.

And I will find her someday...

If this isn't all a load of horseshit that merely demonstrates I haven't yet learned to deal with my emotions.

Ha! That is the million-dollar question, now isn't it?

What do you think, reader?

Profound or horseshit?

Let us know in the comments section below.

XX

Another cold, gloomy afternoon in early January, Mao was driving home from his local rec club after enjoying a spirited tennis match with a friend. Pulling onto his street, the fun of looking for parking in front of his apartment building began. Finding parking in Montréal was a notoriously challenging task, especially in more central and densely-populated neighborhoods like Park-Extension. Usually, barring any kind of extraordinary luck, Mao needed to circle the block at least three times before either finding an open spot, or simply parking his car in a creative (illegal) way. But then, in old Mao's defense, Montréal's parking signage was itself rather creative. Even when Mao did manage to find an open spot, which required a particularly keen eye, he still needed to call on his steely parallel parking skills, and needed to play a little bit of bumper cars, in order to really make the process work.

On the third and final of his three turns around the block, Mao, despite the odds, did actually happen upon a spot being vacated. Hooray! With only three light taps of the gray, beat-up Nissan Versa in front of him, and with only the gentlest bumper kiss of the modified black Mercedes in back of him (a kiss so gentle that the Khanda-shaped air freshener hanging from the Mercedes' rearview mirror didn't even flutter), Mao was in.

With an exhalation of delight, Mao turned the engine off, grabbed his Wilson racquet bag and was ready to sprint into his apartment building as quickly as he could to avoid the cold. But then, he caught a glimpse of something under the windshield wiper of the car now one millimeter from his front bumper. And then, yes, there it was again, under the windshield wiper of the car half a millimeter from his back bumper!

What could it be?

Walking over to the busted-up Nissan, Mao reached over and pulled on the small paper wedged beneath the wiper; wedged, indeed, beneath the wiper of every single car on both sides, up and down the street. With his jacket hood up, his hands quickly stiffening, and his breath visible in the cold, Mao held the card up to his face and read:

THE MYSTIC OF MIMIJAD
Grand Healer and Clairvoyant
Expertise in the all of the following domains: the return of a lost love, professional success, success in school exams/sporting endeavors/contests/competitions, protection against hexes, improvement in general sales/business acumen, bewitchment and manipulation of sworn enemies, protection from black magic and the evil eye, resolution of family conflicts, divorce settlement, success obtaining driver's license, increased confidence, cure of miscellaneous psychological problems including substance and/or gambling addictions, communication with the dead, accurate prediction of major future events, stress relief and overcoming depression, luck in games of chance including lottery, increased size and improved function of sexual organs, etc.
Call for free consultation. The Mystic of Mimijad will use powerful ancient mysticism to help you with any and all problems. **RESULTS GUARANTEED.** *1-800-MIM-IJAD*

After reading the card over twice, Mao scoffed. Truly, he couldn't give cream shit about any of the other ridiculous claims, but was the shyster really claiming he could make his client's dick bigger? Mao shook his head in disappointment. That one was too much.

'How much longer until this lunatic gets sued?' Mao wondered, as he looked up at the windows of Apartment #8. Characteristically, the curtains were drawn. There was absolutely no way of knowing what wacky business was being conducted behind them.

Mao looked down at the card again, and shrugged. At the end of the day, the mystic's business was really none of Mao's. Besides, his hands were getting red from the cold.

So, the polite and respectful Mao carefully replaced the business card where he had found it, shrugged again, and ran into his building to take a hot and well-deserved shower.

XXI

Fragments of Mao's Notes
03/01/2020

Every expression of negativity does the greatest damage at the source. Keep your intentions pure.

All good is chosen.
You can't force someone to be good.
You can force them to follow rules, sure, but they must choose to be good.

I am the most complex being on the face of the universe.
Oh, I mean planet.
Does the universe have a face? I guess the universe could have a face, but that's also kind of a stretch... The planet has a face. Traditionally, the planet has had a face. We've seen it. They have pictures of it. We know the planet has a face. But, the universe... we haven't seen it yet. It eludes us, to this day. This mysterious organism that towers over us and simultaneously engulfs us. It can be overwhelming! But the craziest part of it all is that we all talk about the universe. We all talk about it. We talk about it all the time. But none of us have ever seen its face.

The Cliché

The hero's journey is a metaphor for creation. The artist delves deep within the underworld of himself, where it is dark and perilous, and where there lurk monsters to confront, and, ultimately, to overcome, until he finally returns to the material world from this dangerous journey with something of value, something magic, something sometimes referred to as insight.

Everything sounds ridiculous, until you put it into words properly.

XXII

A hungry Neanderthal ventures out of his cave in search of food. Wandering across the grassy plain, he eventually stumbles upon some strange growths sprouting in the mud. The Neanderthal stops to examine, in his primitive way, these strange, novel organisms. They shoot up in thick white stems topped by hooded pods unlike anything he has ever seen.

Curious, and propelled by hunger, he gathers the pods and heads back in the direction of his cave dwelling, all the while smelling them, wondering if they are good to eat. His grumbling stomach, of course, has already decided he shall take the risk. The trip back home is long, for the caveman has had to venture far beyond the cave in search of his next meal. And so, before he can make it back to his cave, he samples the pods out of irrepressible hunger.

A few hours later, after dark, the cave dweller ventures out of his cave again, to gaze upon the glowing light in the sky he has never before felt compelled to question. What has always seemed to him a mere blurred detail of his surrounding suddenly blazes with ineffable luminescence, haloed by a significance cast in spellbinding waves of light. It looks so beautiful, this cosmic light humbling the simple cave dweller, so radiant and so pure, that he reaches out to it, hearkening to the beacon as a servant does its master, pleading with it to be taken through the beckoning portal and into the beyond.

When the caveman wakes the following morning from a most peaceful slumber, he notices that something has changed. There is a new impulse governing his actions, one that had never been present before. As the sun rises and sets, he slowly begins to understand, in his primitive way, that deep inside of him, the portal still calls.

With this image and sensation become permanently embedded in the deepest fathoms of his being, the Neanderthal sets off on his way to build a ladder to the sky, so that finally and evermore, he could be reunited with that transcendent feeling once again.

XXIII

Mao walks through the quiet, densely forested cross-country ski path, somewhere in the center of Montréal's monolithic Parc Maisonneuve. He is alone. The sun has set, and he is about two hours into the grips of his trip. He's dressed warmly, for this is January in Montréal, after all, and the snow underfoot is bountiful, with the fleecy softness reserved for the freshly fallen. The trees all around seem to whisper, ancestral truths spoken in some ancestral language his human form no longer fully comprehends. Mao hardly notices the colloquy of the conifers, though, for he is rapt in a struggle. He is performing the ritual of 'undoing a knot'. This knot, the knot that has for so long been hindering him, is the primary reason he has undertaken the journey. He has been talking to himself, with only the trees for audience, for over five minutes now. Although, he has no idea of the length of his soliloquy, of course, for one of the most salient characteristics of the journey is one's greatly reduced temporal awareness.

"You're a coward!"

Mao cries out, addressing himself, channeling his inner Al Pacino, a character who seems to be, at this moment, an emblem or surface manifestation of Mao's untapped inner strength. Strength. It is a quality he has been perhaps lacking of late.

"You hide behind your intellectualism because you are afraid to let people see your true vulnerability, your gaping incompleteness, your pathetic uncertainty and doubt!"

Mao really articulates, plowing through his 'p's Pacino style, waving his arms frenetically, occasionally pausing to have a puff at the joint between his right index and middle finger, which serves Pacino as an excellent prop for pointing.

"You inflate your ego like it's a fuckin' life jacket, to keep you from drowning in the ocean of doubt all around you, that you pretend you cannot see. Dumb move buddy, the ocean don't care whether you see it or not, it'll swallow you all the same."

Very theatrical, very passionate. If they could, the trees would surely applaud.

"You elevate yourself to the status of God so that you can cast judgment on others, projecting your insecurities in a futile attempt to discard them. But you can't give them over to others, can you? That's not the way that works."

'Fake it 'til you make it,' they say. Machismo can help a man overcome some weaknesses, though only temporarily. It is much, much more difficult, and yet much, much better to bore down as deeply as possible, in an attempt to find the kernel, the root of the pain. In this metaphor, the 'fake it' would be the machismo, a placeholder for the 'make it', which would be, we suppose, balance.

"You hide behind a veil of vainglory and boasting, to conceal the soft fear of failure that grounds you, that connects you to every mortal soul."

Though, even then, the reward of finding the kernel is not enough to the truly inquisitive mind. To penetrate the kernel, to crack its outer shell, to gaze unabashedly at the ugly, foul, and primal ooze that manifests only symptomatically as emotion, to stare at the ancient history that has written humankind's DNA, that governs our behavior, that is who we are. To gaze unto this quagmire, and to submit to the profound frustration and powerlessness that abounds, the source, the fountainhead of mortal being, is the only known way to release.

"Worst of all, you are a slut, with no morals or scruples, prostituting your thoughts and emotions for the faintest possibility of fame, who would do anything right now for a pen and paper, so that you could write all this down."

Ouf.

For the big finale, Mao drops to his knees and cries. After a few beautiful, purging moments alone with the trees, he looks up to the clear night sky for solace. Reigning majestically from above, the moon is set in the sky like a radiant stone, a luminescent talisman, a portal to the unknown just beyond. It beckons, and like a good, obedient pet, Mao follows.

The Cliché

Later, at a friend's apartment. There was a cab ride, some hysterical laughter, a nightmarish tea party. There were also moments of fairly lucid conversation. 'It comes in waves,' or, so goes the old adage. Sitting at the dining room table, Mao is riding yet another one of these waves, and it is about to crest.

Coins of varied denominations and of varied national origin are strewn across the wooden surface. Off to the side, an elegant hand-carved chess set made in WWII-era Ukraine.

Throughout the entire journey, Mao has felt like everything around him is part of some elaborately-staged scene, and that he is observing its composition with a director's eye. There had been a discussion of symbols, and of the seemingly increased significance of luminescent materials brought on by hallucinogens. The coins provided the perfect convergence of these concepts. After some talk about money, and how financial hardships had placed a great strain on Mao in the past, his friend had gone off somewhere else, entangled in his own cascade. Mao, sitting alone, fingers the beautiful, shining coins, contemplating their ancient symbolic meaning, contemplating power, ambition, greed, and possession. *Possession.* Leaning forward, and laying his head upon his forearm, Mao gazes across the table at the chess set, observing the seamless procession of pieces, perfectly aligned and culminating in the King. *The King. The Father. The Patriarch.* The pursuit of pseudo-invulnerability, the desire to possess all and fear none had cost him love, had cost him genuine connection, had cost him happiness. His palms open involuntarily as the coins fall and clink upon one another, scattering across the surface. He understands. Yes, he understands. He must let go of the pursuit of everything. He must accept that he will never be King.

Suddenly, Mao turns to stare up at the ceiling light fixture. Staring directly into the light, the tears fall silently from his eyes to form a small pool on the table below. He is not in control. He never was. He is not the King. No mortal is.

Submitting the illusion of control entirely, Mao becomes lighter, and lighter, until he is no longer present.

Suddenly turning from the light, his breath quickens. He heaves. He does not hear any words, or discern any language, only the astral vibrations in the light which communicate with him in the ancestral language of the trees. He understands. Primal, prelinguistic understanding washes over him. In proximate, rational terms, what he understands is this:

Submission is okay, letting go is okay. Everything will be alright. Control is an illusion. Everything will be alright. Nothing is that important. Everything will be alright. Of course it will, without question. Everything will be alright. Everything will be alright. Everything is alright.

Eventually, his breathing steadied.

XXIV

Another dark and miserable afternoon in January, Mao was sitting at his kitchen table slurping some delicious soup. It was chicken soup, which his mother had made for him. Mao's mother made excellent chicken soup. Mao was on the mend from a sore throat, which was an ailment he regularly endured at least once a winter. It was a Sunday, and bitterly cold outside. Because he could, Mao had spent the entire day in his pajamas. There was absolutely nothing he needed to do. Later, once he had eaten the soup, he would sit on the couch and read, and then try to come up with something interesting to write down that wasn't an exact regurgitation of what he had just read. This was something Mao had been struggling to do, as his brain felt, in these winter months of boredom, solitude, and sadness, like a frozen wasteland where nothing could possibly grow without extremely dedicated intervention. In this case, extremely dedicated intervention meant paraphrasing the greats who had somehow, all those years ago, found something meaningful to say, and who, all those years ago, had summoned the patience and wherewithal to say it as originally, and as beautifully as they could.

Mao, on the other hand, was content to enjoy his soup while peacefully daydreaming about the contours of A–Z's bottom, and the way it gave just the right amount when impacted by the gentle swing of his open palm. He was remembering just how he would tap that lovely bottom, once, twice, three times, before his rising enthusiasm, mirrored by his rising vigor, would cause A–Z to protest 'Ow!', and he would come to, noticing the red marks he had left on the once-blank canvas.

Ah, if only all blank canvases were as easy to work with!

'Maybe I need a muse,' Mao thought.

It was somewhere along this asinine train of reverie that he became conscious of the hullabaloo coming from across the hall.

Mao rolled his eyes. 'Not this again,' he thought. 'I was finally on to something!'

He dropped his spoon in the soup, wiped his mouth, and laboriously got up to investigate what all the excitement was about.

Mao walked to the heavy chain-locked front door, opened it, and peered across the checkered tiles and yellowing walls of the hall to the infamous Apartment #8. Across the hall, J.C.'s door was open. With the man himself as their escort, two bumbling young men were spilling out of the mystic's apartment, nearly falling over one another as they did. The Mystic of Mimijad stood proudly at the threshold, graciously accepting the shower of praise being poured upon him.

"Thank you, O great one! We are not worthy! Thank you! We are not worthy of your wisdom, great and powerful mystic! You have saved us from our own weakness and stupidity!"

Mao's eyebrows shot up – it seemed to be an involuntary reaction whenever J.C. was around. Both of the mystic's visitors were sharply dressed, wearing expensive-looking denim, polo shirts and designer winter jackets. The avalanche of thanks continued as they proceeded to put on their boots. The Mystic of Mimijad, bless him, took it all in stride. He had his chin up, and was leaning on his Malacca cane in that distinctive pose with both hands cupped around the jackal. He looked about as regal as he did ridiculous.

"Please, please, miboys. This is my work. I always do serious work, and provide serious results for my patients. It was absolutely my pleasure to help you, my dear young men."

Although Mao's door, the door to Apartment #7, was almost entirely open, and although Mao stood there scratching his head in plain sight with his red nose and flannel pajamas, neither the mystic nor his apostles seemed to notice him. The putzes were completely focused on their madman-messiah, hanging on his every word like birds on a wire. Mao watched as Jajùmissu Cá walked right past him, escorting the men across the checkered tiles and yellowing walls of the hall to the stairwell, patting their backs encouragingly, as the dolts continued to desperately thank him with their palms together as though in prayer before the Lord.

When they had descended the first few flights, and were finally out of sight, J.C. turned, and acknowledged Mao with his hands on his waist and a satisfied grin on his face.

Mao tried, but he could not manage to erase the stupefied expression his face seemed to make every time J.C. was around. 'This guy's life is like a cartoon,' Mao thought, 'and the writer's room is full of meth addicts!'

"What in God's good name was that?" Mao asked.

J.C. frowned disapprovingly.

"Why, those were patients of mine, miboy. They came to see me for help with a problem they had. As you can see, I was able to help them very much."

Mao pursed his lips and put his hands on his waist, mimicking the Mimijadian.

"I see that. Seems like quite the problem you solved for them."

J.C. was thoughtful.

"Yes. Quite so, miboy. They are both nice young men, medical students. They were not doing so well with their examinations. They explained that they were having a hard time focusing in class. But they were very smart, and they came to work with me right away. I discovered that the reason they were not doing well was because one of their jealous classmates put a very nasty curse on them! A drowsiness curse. Very, very bad. I gave them medicine to wash their body with. I gave them charms to negate the evil of the curse and keep their minds, bodies, and spirits pure! I removed the curse, miboy, though it took several consultations and a lot of work. They passed their final exams in

December. That is what they came to tell me. They brought me some gifts, and were very grateful to me for my intervention. They have recommended me to friends, and I am getting even more business! You will be seeing a lot more people coming in and out to see the Mystic of Mimijad, miboy."

Mao couldn't believe what he was hearing.

"You're kidding!" he exclaimed.

J.C.'s toothy smile brightened up the hall.

"I never kid, miboy."

J.C. broke out in a hearty laugh.

It seemed so implausible, and yet J.C. seemed so earnest. Mao had just seen those two young men with his own two eyes. As a matter of fact, he could see through the open door across the hall, that sitting on the wooden chest in J.C.'s apartment were two gift-wrapped boxes, one presumably from each of his satisfied 'patients', as he liked to refer to them. He had taken a good look at them. Aside from their incoherent babbling, the pair seemed normal enough. By the looks of their clothes, their builds, and their postures, they seemed well put together, even.

But then, it just couldn't be. There had to be something Mao was missing.

Maybe J.C. had staged the whole thing. He was a weirdo... Mao couldn't put it past him.

But then, what was the point of staging something like that? What was the upside? Just to convince Mao of his legitimacy?

That seemed too farfetched, even for the Mystic of Mimijad. But then, could this man really have the magic powers he claimed?

As though reading Mao's mind, J.C.'s eyes narrowed as he tilted his head forward, tapping his Malacca cane against the frame of Mao's Apartment #7 door.

"And you, young man, when will you come and see the Mystic of Mimijad? Do not tell me you are still unconvinced of his abilities."

J.C.'s predatory instinct was good. He had Mao where he wanted him.

"Just out of curiosity, how much does the Mystic of Mimijad charge to remove a drowsiness curse? Is there a flat rate, or does it vary by hex?"

J.C. smiled conspiratorially.

"Ah, miboy, it certainly does depend on the nature of the curse. Some are much more difficult to remove, I'm afraid."

Mao watched him skeptically, but J.C's movements were self-assured.

"And those two nimrods, they really passed their medical exams?"

The mystic laughed heartily.

"Of course!"

Mao nodded thoughtfully. But then, something occurred to him.

"How did you figure out that it was a drowsiness curse keeping them from focusing in class? How did you know it wasn't because a werewolf took a dump on their front porch, or because their mother-in-law sprinkled chlorine in their cornflakes, or something else entirely?"

Jajùmissu Cá gave a start of surprise, and recoiled indignantly, as though Mao had said something shockingly distasteful.

"Why, I cannot discuss that with you, miboy. That is subject to patient-mystic confidentiality! However, what I can say, the boys were very satisfied with my work. They certainly got their money's worth!"

Again that hearty chuckle.

"For you, my friend, I cannot tell without a consultation how much of my help you will really need. But, an hour of my time, I will give to you, as a show of good faith, for just..." Mao waited patiently as Jajùmissu Cá's brain whizzed, estimating how much money he could squeeze without losing his mark, "twenty dollars! The Mystic of Mimijad is all about helping people, and I know you need my help young man. I can smell it on you. It is the smell of death. And it only gets stronger, miboy, every time we cross paths."

Mao took it in. It seemed kind of reasonable. At the very least, he'd be entertained for an hour, right? We mean, what could one even buy for twenty Canadian dollars these days?

"Okay, sure," Mao said.

J.C. did his best to hide his surprise.

"Sure?"

Mao shrugged.

"Yeah, sure. I'll take you up on your offer. An hour of your time, twenty dollars. I think it might be nice to speak with the Mystic of Mimijad and to hear his assessment of my situation."

J.C.'s face lit up with that toothy smile once more.

"Wonderful! I am glad to hear it, young man. You will be glad you did. But I must warn you: you must enter the process with an open heart, and an open mind. Your defenses will come down, and you will be made to feel vulnerable in a way you may not have ever felt before. It may frighten you, but you must trust in my guidance in order for us to truly gaze into the depths of your soul. We will journey deep into the shadows together. Then, and only then, will I be able to cure you of your troubles."

Mao, in his pajamas, nodded and yawned.

"Nice."

"Indeed! It is settled. Next weekend, Saturday, at eight o'clock in the evening. I will prepare for you, young man. You shall dine, and afterwards we shall carefully explore the folds of your psyche. It shall be a taxing experience, so be sure to eat well, but no cloven hooves! And definitely no shellfish. Oh, and make sure to wash right before coming, miboy. It is necessary to cleanse any additional toxins lingering on the surface. They may interfere with our probing."

Mao nodded again, and with a flourish of his fuchsia robes, J.C. turned, crossed the checkered tiles and yellowing walls of the hall, and disappeared behind the closed door of Apartment #8. Mao stood there for a moment watching the door, wondering what he had just got himself into.

But then he remembered he had some soup waiting for him and that it was probably getting cold.

XXV

Being single sure does leave a guy with a lot of extra time on his hands. For Mao, the majority of this 'found time' was spent reading, playing sports, or hanging out with friends. And sometimes, on weekends when the weather was bad, and after Mao had maybe had a few day drinks, he liked to entertain himself, and his buddies if they were around, by indulging in the nostalgia of a deliciously absurd crank call.

Drrrrring... drrrrring.

"Bonjour-Hi, Boulangerie Lola, comment puis-je vous aider – how can I help you?"

Indulge us, patient and docile reader, just a brief moment for clarification.

Bonjour-Hi, thoughtful and cultured reader, is the standard 'franglais' greeting one is supposed to lead with in Montréal, if one is Anglophone. Otherwise, it would just be *Bonjour.* It would never, however, be just *Hi.* Neither, tolerant and wise reader, would it ever be *Hi-Bonjour.* No one, and we mean *no one,* would ever dare to make the injudicious error of putting the *Hi* before the *Bonjour.* In Québec, this kind of linguistic malfeasance is dealt with swiftly and fiercely. The law offers little reprieve for hooligans who besmirch the sanctity and magnanimity of the

The Cliché

Bonjour-Hi. What's more, noble and kind reader, is that there wouldn't be a lawyer in all the land (of Québec) that would in any way be able to help you if you were ever found, even accidentally, to have spoken more English words than French words in any sort of public or even private setting. Oh, that's right. And if you happened to be a business owner, well, you'd have an even bigger target on your back. Hell, if one wanted one's business to thrive, we'd recommend doing away with the English entirely. Clinging onto that nasty, antiquated language could only bring trouble. One never knew when Québec's secret language police would strike.

And so, it was because of these facts of (Québec) life that these clearly English business owners had opted to call their bakery Boulangerie Lola, rather than Lola's Bakery, and answered the phone with the customary *Bonjour-Hi* expected of a business that catered to a ninety-seven percent Anglophone clientele. This particular *boulangerie* had been open for over ten years, and was located around the corner from Mao's childhood home. Mao thought it was a good bakery. Though for years, Boulangerie Lola's employees were some of Mao's favorite crank call victims.

Today's employee was male, and sounded eager to please. It had been a long time since Mao had crank called Boulangerie Lola. Years, really, and he was glad to have been offered up such a gullible and servile-sounding employee for his triumphant return.

"*Bonjour-Hi, Boulangerie Lola, comment puis-je vous aider* – how can I help you?"

"Oh, hello!"

Mao affects a stuffy, 'extremely busy businessman' voice that is colored by just a trace of impatience, and as thick a British accent as he can muster.

"I have a birthday party coming up and I am shopping for a suitable cake."

Ah, the birthday cake order! One of Mao's favorite routines...

"Oh, yes, of course! Anything in particular, sir?"

The employee's voice is especially cheery. Mao estimates at least fifteen minutes of torture before he gets hung up on.

"Quite particular indeed! I should like one exquisite Batman cheesecake, if I may."

The employee barrels on cheerily.

"Alrighty, well that shouldn't be a problem sir! We can do a variety of Batman cakes, and a cheesecake shouldn't be a problem."

"Did you hear me man? It has to be exquisite!"

There is a pause, before the employee lets out an uncomfortable laugh.

"Oh, yes, of course. I assure you, all our cakes are exquisite, sir. How many children will be at the party?"

Mao unleashes his most theatrical 'affronted nobleman' grunt.

"Children? Who said anything about children? I think there's been a misunderstanding."

The employee's tone is adjusted, colored with the appropriate apologetic servility.

"Oh, I'm so sorry, sir. I just presumed the cake was for a children's party since you asked for a Batman cake."

"I asked, my good man, for an exquisite Batman *cheesecake*. You'll do well to listen more carefully henceforth."

There is an awkward pause. Mao waits patiently.

"Oh, right. Of course, sir. A Batman cheesecake."

"Now listen here you sod, I won't have any of this from you. Why would you presume that cake would be for children? I dare say I'd like to speak with your manager."

The cretin spinelessly backpedals.

"Oh, no! Sir, I assure you I did not mean any offence. I am sure we do not need to get the manager involved?"

Mao's voice softens.

"Oh, well, alright then. No more of that nonsense, then, Johnson."

"My name is Habib, s-"

Mao cuts him off.

"There'll be no more of that, Johnson, not until you've taken my order to my satisfaction. Now, as I was saying, this lovely specimen of a cake will be for *my* party. I absolutely need to have a magnificent Batman cheesecake for the event. The idea came to me in a vision. I saw it – the most magnificent cake being tabled and cut in front of all of my friends, as all of them cheered and applauded, or looked on in envy, and I simply have to make it a reality. Tell me, Johnson, is that such a crime? Is it indeed a crime for a grown man to spend his hard-earned money on an exquisitely magnificent Batman cheesecake to enjoy with all his friends on his birthday? Is it, Johnson?"

The employee is as patient and apologetic as ever.

"Not at all, sir. My apologies. It of course makes no difference to me who the cake is for. It was silly of me to assume."

"You know how the expression goes, don't you Johnson? About assuming, and making an ass of yourself?"

Habib, the employee, chuckles.

"Oh, yes. I know the expression."

"But you're not an ass, are you Johnson?"

Habib chuckles again.

"Oh, no sir."

"Very good. Now, about the cake."

"Oh, yes, of course, we can prepare a Batman cheesecake that you and all your friends will love, no problem. How many people will the cake be for? We offer the choice between several Batman images for the top of the cake."

"Images? Listen here you mountebank, I said no such thing about wanting any images on my cake. I thought you were better than this, Johnson. Do you take me for a fool, or are you merely a common swindler? No, that simply won't do. Could you imagine? If I tabled and cut a cake with an *image* of Batman on top, in front of all of my friends? Why, I'd be reduced to the country club laughing stock! Listen carefully Johnson; I need the cheesecake to be *shaped* like Batman. Are you understanding me man?"

"You want a cake *shaped* like Batman?"

Habib is incredulous. He has never even considered that a cake could be *shaped* like Batman.

"Precisely, you servile prat. However, there is one small specification, though I'm sure it won't cause any trouble. The cake must be shaped like the *Christian Bale* Batman. Mark my word Michaels, if my glorious cake is in the shape of any of the other *weak, pretentious,* and *downright unbelievable* renditions of Batman, I will personally get into my Lamborghini Aventador, floor the gas pedal thus engaging all seven hundred and fifty horsepower at my disposal, screech into the parking lot of your place of business, storm through your front door, and show everyone in the store, both employees and patrons, the preposterous piece of *garbage* you tried to have me table and cut in front of all my friends. And that's not all, Johnson. Then! Then, I will stand there as you wallow in the shame of your miserable and pathetic cakesmanship as everyone in the store points their finger and laughs at you, until you finally shed a tear. And then I'll lift and throw the entire lousy cream-shit excuse for a cake directly into your stupid face! Do I make myself crystal clear, Johnson?"

Habib is impressively unfazed.

"Oh, yes, very clear. Sir, my name is Habib, and although you sound like a lovely man, I don't think we can make you a cheesecake shaped like Batman."

A lovely man! That one almost gets Mao to break.

"The *Christian Bale* Batman! You need to be writing these details down, you simpleton, so you won't forget!"

Habib chuckles.

"Please calm down."

"How can I calm down? You've been known to be forgetful, Johnson."

"Sir! Please. I will not be able to make you a cake shaped like Christian Bale, or any of the other Batmans, I'm afraid."

"No Batman, you say?"

"No Batman. Unless you want an image of Batman on top of a normal, round cheesecake, we can't do it."

Habib is just about done with him. Mao calms himself down, steadies the line.

"Well. That is really quite disappointing."

"I'm sorry, sir."

God bless him for having the wherewithal, at this stage in the proceedings, to call Mao 'sir'.

"I've got to say Johnson, I'm rather crestfallen. Someone referred me to your shop, and told me you had a team of wizard bakers who would surely be able to satisfy my needs."

"I'm sorry, sir. I would really love to help you. Perhaps a different kind of cake?"

"Well, I suppose the Batman cheesecake idea is out the window. I should have known. I'll admit, the idea was a bit farfetched... Say, does your shop make a good tiramisu?"

Habib is back on board.

"Oh, a very good tiramisu, sir. One of our specialties. Our customers love it."

"Very well, then. I am willing to concede to a Spiderman tiramisu, so long as it is shaped like the *Tobey Maguire* Spiderman, and none of those other *weak, pathetic-*"

That was when ol' Habib had enough, and hung up.

Mao was right, just about fifteen minutes!

XXVI

Fragments of Mao's Notes
05/01/2020

The work is all internal. If you believe you're a tragic figure, then it's a self-fulfilling prophecy.

What is the difference between being happy and being emulsified?

Compassion is the essence of a spiritual life.

XXVII

Reader.

Sweet, darling reader.

We would like to seize this moment to express our gratitude to you for having made it this far. We realize, noble and agreeable reader, that as you are consuming us in the finite, novelistic, narrative form, you understand that we are nearing the end of our beautiful time together. And as sad as that does make us, we are absolutely thrilled that you have been able to join us for the ride. Never in a million years did we expect to be graced with a reader as wonderfully tolerant of perversion and madness as you clearly are. So really, truly, from the depths of our disembodied metaphor for a heart, thank you.

You know, as much as Mao loved the Arctic Monkeys, he hadn't even been listening to their music for *that* long. Coincidentally, he had only really gotten into them right before meeting A–Z. Perhaps that association, between the discovery of great music and the quicksilver of young love is what really solidified his love of the band. In the early days, when he and A–Z were just fooling around or 'seeing each other', he would listen to the Monkeys' music on the drive over every time he went to pick her up. This offered him a lot of time to develop the connection between the two, as A–Z lived rather far away from Mao, and she didn't drive. Those crosstown drives sound tracked by the Monkeys and colored by his natural desire for A–Z caused the two sensations to become melded into one oh so sweet emotion.

Mao often opted for the album *Humbug*, as the adrenaline of the opener 'My Propeller' would always get him going, as he did his best to channel his youthful nerves into a cheerful exuberance he tried to pass off as charm. It was the first time in a while he had felt that pit in his stomach, that visceral desire to come off as nonchalant as possible, so as to make a good enough impression to, if all went well, get A–Z to 'spin' his 'propeller'.

Their early dates were a lot of fun, marked by their clear physical, emotional, and intellectual chemistry. She exuded confidence, they had a lot of overlapping interests, and she was just the right amount of crazy. Mao's type. However, it quickly became apparent that the two were at very different places in the trajectory of their lives. A–Z was fairly fresh out of her fourth, fifth, or sixth relationship running, and felt in many ways that she was headed straight for her nineteenth nervous breakdown, while Mao was caught with his pants down, called off the bench and thrown straight into the action, at core incompetent, but leading the way forward nonetheless, blinders on, confidently and repeatedly walking straight into walls. The first few months they dated were a drama of shared roles: hesitation contrasted by passionate declarations that kept it all from slipping away.

Ultimately, the two decided the proverbial leap of faith was one worth taking, but not until they reached their turning point.

Alright, so now you see. There is actually a reason we've been harping on about the Arctic Monkeys this whole time. It's because of the turning point, and the integral role the Arctic Monkeys played in that story. As far as Mao was concerned, the turning point that led him to where he was in early 2020 – sad, broken, and creatively constipated – was entirely Alex Turner and the Arctic Monkeys' fault.

Reader, human memory operates in funny, mysterious ways. We like to think of it as a sort of retrospective story machine, connecting dots and reinterpreting chance happenings to create the neat narrative mortals call their 'past'. Omens, dear reader. It has always fascinated us how some people, mostly those 'creative' or 'spiritual' types, could interpret certain arbitrary events or coincidental moments in such a way that imbues them with underserved, narrative-driving meaning. Omens, dear reader, and milestones. They enable the mystically inclined to look back at the days of their lives, piecing them together in such a way that fits neatly into a palatable story arc, and which helps the lost individual blindly navigating the chaos of his or her life to find providence in his or her entirely random and petty existence. Omens, dear reader, and signs of divine guidance. It was just one of these omens that Mao used to explain the cause of his and A–Z's split. Or rather, this cardinal moment was meant to explain how the two were never meant to date in the first place. Omens, dear reader, omens! While emotions are lodged deep in the heart, omens are lodged quite firmly in the brain. Though they may seem like much, much more, they are often just paltry defense mechanisms used to rationalize meaning and purpose out of chaos, and to fight against the cold, hard reality that everything is incidental, and that all of man's best laid plans can come crashing down in a spectacular blaze of glory at any moment. Omens, dear reader, are beacons filled with prophetic importance. They guide mortals through the madness of life, providing the light that shines the way to happiness...

In 2018, Mao and A–Z had just begun dating. It was truly an idyllic scene. The two of them just worked, you know? They were the kind of pair that outsiders looked in on with approval of what seemed to be genuine happiness. But the thing that people on the outside couldn't see was the pressure Mao would put on A–Z. Why? Well, if we're frank, it can probably be chalked up to inexperience. Mao had some experience with lust, though none of it translated to love. He was not prepared to deal with the feelings that A–Z evoked in him. He squeezed too tight. He demanded too much. He wriggled un-sanctimoniously for control over the ephemeral matters of the heart.

And so, in a fit of self-sabotage, Mao gave A–Z the ultimatum.

It was just around the same time that this silly struggle was taking place that the Arctic Monkeys were set to headline the famous Osheaga Music and Arts Festival on Saturday, August 4th, 2018, as part of the North American leg of their Tranquility Base Hotel & Casino World Tour. At the time of its release, Mao wasn't sure how he felt about the album. It was weird, and he hadn't had the time to process it yet. Also, unsurprisingly, he was broke. Also, A-Z was broke, so she wasn't going. So, naturally, Mao decided he wouldn't go to the show either.

However, in an unexpected twist that fateful afternoon of Saturday, the 4th of August, 2018, Mao had found himself leaving A-Z's place just after breaking up with her. And why did he do that? He broke up with her, because she did not want to commit to their being together.

Mao, having yet to learn the valuable lesson that to force is to break, was driving home a mess of emotions, really, unable to understand what he just did, or why he did it, and was trying to convince himself he did not make a huge mistake. Of course, he was struggling with that last bit. So, he called a few friends up. They were, unsurprisingly, on their way to the famous Osheaga Music and Arts Festival, to watch Alex Turner and the Arctic Monkeys headline the festival and lead the crowd to the promised land of rock n' roll euphoria. The Monkeys were set to take the stage at nine o'clock. Mao looked at the clock. It was three in the afternoon.

It did not take much to convince Mao to join in, and he did. He met his friends at the Berri-UQAM Metro station in the heart of the city, and the squad took the yellow line to the Parc Jean Drapeau station, which led out directly into the beautiful nature park serving as Osheaga's outdoor venue. By four o'clock, Mao was hyped and had completely forgotten about A–Z. He was approaching scalpers, eager to land himself a ticket to see the Monkeys, cut loose, and forget about A–Z for now and evermore.

However, there was a hitch in his simple plan. Remember how Mao was broke? Well, Osheaga tickets weren't cheap. And especially not when a band like the Arctic Monkeys were headlining, so that scalpers could resell the sold-out tickets at three times their face value. He approached three, four, then five scalpers, all to the same effect. He just couldn't afford the ticket. The price was exorbitant.

By five-thirty, Mao's friends (who all had tickets already) had abandoned him at the entrance, where Mao was left feeling more and more depressed with every passing minute. The attempt to get A–Z off his mind was proving to be a failure, and he was left with only his emptiness and remorse. At six o'clock, he decided to call it quits and head back home.

The next day, after a difficult night's sleep, Mao was feeling a little down. His friends were all posting on social media, raving about how great the Arctic Monkeys were, and he felt like he had really missed out on something special. In the afternoon, on the verge of calling her, he received a call from A-Z. He went to see her, they talked it out, and they made up.

Omens, dear reader, omens.

You see, in Mao's mind, there was no doubt that had he gotten into that concert and seen the Monkeys, he would have been on cloud nine. He would not have had the tough, remorse-bitten night he had. He would not have been feeling down the next day, but instead would have felt incredible, joining in on the magical social media afterglow of a spectacular evening with the Monkeys at Osheaga. Thus, he would obviously have ignored A-Z's call. In his mind, had he seen the Monkeys on that fateful day of Saturday, August 4th, 2018, he would never have seen A-Z again. They would never have fallen so deeply in love, and he would never have had to go through the searing heartache that ensued as a result. What he would have done, instead, was write another book. Indeed, because of that one bad decision not to go into debt to see a cool band, and the ensuing bad decision to answer a phone call from the woman he was crazy about, he now had no book, no woman, no happiness, and no prospect for any of these things anywhere on the horizon.

Omens, dear reader, omens.

Isn't it funny how mortals can look back on things, on events in their lives, and see not what happened, but see instead their own biased, personalized, skewed interpretation? Let us be clear: Mao had no choice in the matter. He, like all mortals, was simply an agent of fate. Clearly, he was not meant to see the Arctic Monkeys that day. He was meant to date A–Z, and she was meant to break his heart. Everything unravels in the only way it can. And the only way to gracefully navigate the bump and grind of a human life is to accept one's powerlessness to the whims of chance, thus finding the flexibility and lightness of heart to change, and grow with the times.

Seeing the Arctic Monkeys that day might have saved Mao a lot of pain. However, there's something to be said for pain. Sometimes, pain is necessary. Some, possessing ineffable wisdom, have called it humanity's greatest teacher. Some, less ascetic, have had the blessing to find the insight and realization of what wonderful serendipity it is to be hurt in such a way that must ultimately make you stronger. And some, unfortunately, are doomed to wander the blind alley of ignorance.

Though, it is never too late for one to alter the path, and orient oneself towards the light...

XXVIII

Fragments of Mao's Notes
07/01/2020

Jim Morrison in 'The End' says the kids are all insane, and this, one would presume, was revolutionary at the time. It was revolutionary because the kids were breaking all of the chains, and discovering freedom from tradition and expectation and norms. Nowadays, the chains have all been broken. When someone says "the kids are all insane," the postmodern world replies: "so what?"

Postmodern life is a bionic hand with the answers to everything except how to be happy.

I guess the idea I wanted to convey was basically something along the lines of the fact that the subjectivism (or relativism) that arises from postmodern tenets, as well as the idea that one must suffer for one's art, are both untenable, or at least incompatible with happiness, in spite of the fact that these ideas are both supported by fairly good logic. And I wanted to propose an antidote... though I haven't found one yet. But then, all this crap keeps getting in the way, like character and setting, and plot. But I mean, without all that stuff, what would I have? An essay? Who the heck would read an essay?

The concept of 'story' precedes the story of God. And that is a creation. Our desire to create, to make the idea manifest in reality, to transcend the gap between the conscious and the physical, is our desire to create each and every one of ourselves in the image of God. Or, rather, to create Gods in the image of ourselves... as we might wish to be.

The expression 'all's well that ends well' is a funny one because nothing ever really 'ends', does it? Aside from the individual, pretty much everything kind of just... continues. And so, the real expression, for the sake of accuracy, should just be 'all's well'. Because it is.

XXIX

Mao tossed his backpack in the trunk and walked over to the passenger side of the blue roadster. He was glad to see the sky was clear, and he delighted in the feeling of the crisp, fresh air on his skin. Though it was quite cold, the December sun was strong and bright. It was a rare day, Mao thought, of the choice few one would feel comfortable calling a beautiful winter's day. Filling his lungs with a deep pull of the clean, cool air, Mao opened the door, tapped his boot against the doorframe to loosen the excess snow from his heel, and eased himself into the soft, Italian leather embrace of the passenger seat.

Opposite him, in the driver's seat, Ricardo was primed for the road with his black leather gloves on (matching the black leather interior of the car) and his dark Gucci glasses. The pair had just finished up a rigorous leg day at Fit for Eternity, followed by an even more rigorous exchange of complaints, vulgar remarks, and general stupidity in the locker room, while the men showered and changed. The two were now headed to a nearby bistro - the one that Ricardo had been raving about inexhaustibly the entire time they were squatting.

"Hey buddy, you can push this button if you want. It'll turn the ass-warmer on."

Mao scanned the sleek cherry wood finishing of the console, found the button Ricardo was referring to, and clicked the heater on. Ricardo shifted into first and pressed down on the gas. The Maserati responded with a gentle rumble, and the men were off.

Ricardo went on:

"Be careful, though. It packs a real punch. You can't keep it on too long."

Although it was undeniably a beautiful day, Mao reflected with a shiver, it was still December, and it was getting pretty cold outside. It was still not quite January, or February cold yet, but it was getting there. December was only just a taste of things to come.

"Gee, thanks, Rick."

Mao leaned back in the comfortable seat and relaxed. Before even a minute or two he could already feel the seat warmers at work. With his eyes glazing over in delight, Mao looked over at Ricardo, who was focused on the road ahead.

"Simply out of curiosity, and believe me, I do appreciate your generosity with the ass-warmer and all, it feels very nice. But, out of curiosity, you mentioned I shouldn't keep it on too long. Why is that?"

Mao was fooling around, teasing Ricardo, carrying the spirit of the locker room repartee into the car. Ricardo, however, no longer seemed to be in the mood. He shot Mao a serious look from behind his dark Gucci glasses, and replied bluntly:

"If you leave the ass-warmer on too long it will burn your chestnuts."

Mao snorted.

"What?"

He was laughing, but Ricardo, despite the words that had just come out of his mouth, was not. He gave Mao another stoic look. Mao looked back at him, smirking. Mao hated to admit it, but the dark Gucci glasses Ricardo liked to wear behind the wheel did, admittedly, add a certain cachet, or credibility to Ricardo's otherwise ridiculous comments.

"What, what? You don't believe me? You think I talk for nothing?"

There was a hint of irritation in Ricardo's tone. Mao grinned. Getting the other riled up for sport was the cornerstone of their friendship.

"I never said that. Can't a guy ask for an explanation? Is this Stalin's Russia or Trudeau's Canada over here?"

Ricardo looked over ironically.

"Just listen to me for once without being a smart ass, alright? They warned me at the dealership. The expression the salesman used was 'roast your chestnuts.' As in, 'sir, be careful not to keep the ass-warmer on too long, because it's quite powerful, and if you do leave it on too long, it can, and more than likely will roast your chestnuts. There was a class action lawsuit, and now I am legally required to inform every customer that walks through our door.'

That's what he said to me. And now I'm telling you. So, do what you want."

Mao kept laughing, still unconvinced.

"They called it an 'ass-warmer' at the Maserati dealership?"

Ricardo shook his head and sighed.

"But more importantly, was the salesman who gave you this warning wearing a monocle?"

Ricardo grit his teeth.

"Because, if you cannot confirm that the salesman was wearing a monocle, I do not see how I can be expected to take any of his advice seriously."

Ricardo made no reply.

The two sat in silence for a moment, before Mao changed tack.

"Besides, even if what you say is true, I still don't see what the big deal is. Everyone *prefers* their chestnuts roasted."

That one got Ricardo to crack. Mao was still laughing, laughing at Ricardo – Mao thought that with his stupid haircut, his sleek black coat and his black glasses, Ricardo looked like an extra who didn't quite make the cut for *The Matrix*. Ricardo began laughing, too – the idea of Mao's hardheadedness leading to infertility suddenly struck him as hilarious.

"Free birth control, bud. Now all you need to do is make enough money to drive a car like this."

It was still bright out, despite the fact that the short winter's day was already beginning to fade into the late afternoon. Under the sun, the streets of Villeray glared with the runoff from the soft and quickly melting December snow. Ricardo, however, drove as if he hardly noticed, or if he did, could not be bothered by the conditions. Although built for speed, Mao figured the Maserati was likely designed with the mostly dry highways of the Italian coastline in mind, or at least closer to mind than the slushy, slippery streets of wintertime Montréal. That being said, he had to concede that the car, so far, was handling Ricardo's aggressive disregard for safety with grace. It probably helped that the car was equipped with winter tires that cost more than Mao's whole car did, even with a full tank of gas.

But, still.

As Mao mulled it over, his chances of dying, that is, Ricardo, still driving like a psychotic with a death wish, took it upon himself to pick up the lagging small talk.

"So, how's the writing going, babe?"

That got Mao's attention. He looked over at Ricardo and raised an eyebrow. He hated it when Ricardo called him babe, but he was too surprised by the question to be annoyed. It wasn't *at all* like Ricardo to take interest in his creative pursuits.

"First of all, do not call me babe, you caveman. Even if your wildest dreams came true and I did turn out to be gay, I would have much better options than to date someone as dumb and ugly as you. Second of all, since when do you ask me about my writing?"

Mao's words were dripping with skepticism, though Ricardo, rarely aware of anyone but himself, didn't seem to notice.

"Sorry, babe. Won't happen again."

He smiled at Mao, and pressed on.

"Oh, come on. I've always taken interest in your writing. You're my friend for Pete's sake! I always ask about your writing."

None of this, of course, was even remotely true, but it is a testament to repetition's power as a tool of persuasion that Mao was frowning, stirring up the dregs of his memory to recall just one other time that Ricardo might have ever asked him anything even obliquely related to his writing.

"Have you written anything new? Anything you might possibly want to show me?"

Ricardo's cajoling was making inroads into Mao's defenses. Though this was all momentarily suspended, as Ricardo hooked a sudden right onto Rue Jarry without so much as tapping the brakes. As the Maserati veered into the turn, Mao was momentarily winded by the sensation of every vital organ in his midsection crashing against his rib cage. Though the thought flashed by as only the briefest of flickers, as Mao's conscious mind was summoned by the very real danger into full immersion in the present moment, he, later, upon reflection, found himself seriously doubting whether Ricardo could have made out another car, or even a pedestrian, should one have been unfortunate enough to have been crossing at that time, with the blinding glare from the wet road and from the angle at which he recklessly plunged the Maserati into that turn. The dark Gucci glasses glimmered in the light undaunted, revealing nothing, though no doubt contributing to the boneheaded bravado required for a maneuver of that magnitude. Luckily for all parties involved, anyway, there were none unfortunate enough to have been crossing just then. And just like that, the rumbling roadster was headed east, towards Rue Saint Denis.

As his jaw and sphincter gradually loosened, Mao looked over at Ricardo inquisitively. Ricardo noticed this time, and lowered his dark glasses, revealing his maniacal eyes.

"What? Can't a friend take interest?"

Mao lingered a moment longer, wondering how likely it was that a comment on

Ricardo's driving would fall on deaf ears, and then decided to save his breath. He needed the oxygen. He looked ahead and shrugged it off.

"Sure. I mean if you really want to see what I've been working on, I guess I can read you something from my notes."

It was Ricardo's turn to raise an eyebrow.

"Your notes?"

"Yeah, my notes."

It was Mao's turn to be a little irritated.

"I've been writing some stuff in my phone's notes. I feel like a lot of writers must. It's convenient. The phone is always with me, anyway. I may as well do something useful with it, right?"

Ricardo made a face.

"Writing a book on a phone. If that doesn't scream 'millenial', I don't know what does."

They had reached the corner of Rue Saint Denis, where Ricardo smoothly brought the car to a stop at a red light.

"Well, alright. I'm nothing if not open-minded."

Mao decided to let that one slide, too. Ricardo was about as open-minded as a slice of processed cheese.

But despite the volatility, Mao was enjoying the ride.

"Okay. I'd like to see what you think of these little excerpts first. Then maybe I'll show you something a little longer."

Ricardo was getting impatient. He hated waiting for red lights. And often, in less busy parts of town, or at less exposed times of day, didn't.

"I said alright, kid. Get on with it already. You're losing your audience."

The light turned green and the car lurched forward. Mao smirked, and clicked the ass-warmers off. Ricardo was right; his chestnuts were on fire.

"Okay, here goes."

Mao scrolled through his phone, and cleared his throat.

"Larry, there's something I need to tell you! You see, it's like this: I saw Big Rhonda at the store earlier, and she told me that your mom just joined Q Anon. I'm really sorry."

Ricardo looked over at Mao, lowered his glasses, and cackled like a hyena.

"You're retarded dude."

Mao rolled his eyes.

"You have a filthy mouth, Rick. Someone needs to wash it with soap."

Ricardo cackled even louder. He lifted his right arm from the gearshift and flexed.

"And who do you propose is going to do that?"

Mao smirked. Despite Ricardo's inappropriate language, he was glad that he was laughing. The jokes were landing.

"We both know I could kick your ass."

Ricardo cracked the driver's window.

"That comment's even dumber than your Q Anon bit."

Mao scrolled down a little further.

"Here's another one for you. Ready?"

Ricardo smiled. His laughter had even remedied his reckless driving.

Is there anything it can't cure?

"Yes, please. Read me some more from your notes of a deranged young man."

'Is that a Bukowski reference?' Mao wondered. 'Couldn't be! This inbred monkey doesn't read.'

Still, the comment gave Mao confidence. He affected a southern accent:

"'I saw her the other day by the fruit stand. She seems nice.'

'Oh, yeah, who's this?'

'The new girl in town. What was her name again? Ah, yes. Kombucha Wildflower. She's mighty pretty.'

'Komwatcha Whoflower? Who the heck is that?'

'Oh, you know her, Willie.'

'I do?'

He leaned in conspiratorially.

'You know... she's the vegan,' he whispered, as Willie's eyes widened in terror."

Ricardo was howling.

"*OH! HAHAHA!* Magnificent! You're positively disturbed!"

Ricardo's howls were infectious, and Mao began laughing too.

Then suddenly, the Maserati came to a halt. The pair had arrived. Mao looked out the window and saw the posh dining room through the glass, with, of course, the accompanying line to get in. The sign read: *Pince*.

The car moved on slowly, as Ricardo began looking for parking. This was always an endeavour on Rue Saint Denis, especially where the bistro was located, near Rachel. The popular downtown area was dense with commerce, and especially with restaurants.

"Maybe I am disturbed. I've been experimenting with a different way of writing these days. It seems to be coming to me in the shape of these vignettes. Maybe it's because everyone has such a short attention span these days. I guess I'm no different. It's the bloody phones."

Mao brought his phone up to his face to examine, and then threw it down onto the seat theatrically.

"Everyone knows these phones mess everything up, destroying human relationships and blunting us to social cues, but they're just so goddamn addictive. Can you even imagine not watching porn literally whenever the hell you want? Or somehow valuing casual, human exchanges with strangers, or with the opposite sex without all this weirdness? This... neurosis? This fixation on electronically pre-qualified compatibility, whether romantic or political, that so obscures the simple fact that true compatibility is found in a shared smile, not in a swipe, or the double-tap of a picture on a screen? I don't know. It's not my best work, but I'm riffing. What I'm trying to get at is the love, man. It seems like the well is a little drier than it should be. And that's all I want to get across in this book. And I'm just trying to figure out how. I am figuring it out, I think. Slowly."

Ricardo had a little laugh to himself.

"Alright then, Mao. You're a real character."

Mao was being serious. The laughs were alright, but his outburst had been genuine. He picked up his phone and scrolled a little more. Then, he shook his head, locked the screen, and returned the device to his pocket.

"You know what, Rick? I actually do have something a little longer I could show you, if you're into it. It's in my backpack. I printed it out and have been meaning to get some eyes on it."

Ricardo was still scanning the side of the road for an open spot.

"Okay, sure," he replied distractedly. "You know, I can't believe a place like *Pince* doesn't have a valet."

Mao was deep in thought. The prospect of showing Ricardo the little piece he was working on electrified him.

"I'll show you at the restaurant if you like."

"Yeah. I'd like that."

Ricardo spotted a neat little space between a Honda Fit and a Land Rover. It was tight, but one didn't get very far driving in Montréal without developing exceptional parallel parking skills.

"You gotta give me your honest opinion though."

Mao's anxiety betrayed him. As Ricardo lined his car up to execute the parallel, he looked over at Mao half impatiently, and half sardonically.

"When do I ever give you anything but my honest opinion?"

Mao considered the question.

"I guess you're right."

In the ensuing silence, Mao could hear the snow crunching beneath the Maserati's tires as Ricardo backed the car into the spot.

"By the way, Rick, I've been meaning to ask you: how are things going with Keith?"

Ricardo ignored the question until he had done it – somehow tucked his car into the spot without so much as a love tap on either the bumper in front, or the bumper in back, and with snow on the ground, back wheel drive and only millimeters to spare. Mao noticed this, and applauded in admiration. Ricardo kept both hands on the heated wheel and nodded in acknowledgement of the well-deserved praise.

"Rick?"

Ricardo sighed.

"Keith? It's over. We're done."

Mao was a little surprised to hear that. The pair had only been dating for a few weeks, but he had seen them together a few times at Fit for Eternity. They seemed to have a lot in common. They seemed, to Mao, like a natural fit.

"Ah, man, I'm really sorry to hear that. What happened?"

Ricardo took off his glasses, and stored them in the small overhead compartment above the rearview. He looked Mao in the eyes.

"What happened? I caught him butt-naked with our Amazon deliveryman Jérémie. In our bed, and on the thousand-count

Egyptian cotton sheets the bastard delivered into my hands just the week before. What a goddamn cliché."

Though it was hard for him to fathom, Mao, for a second, actually felt bad for Ricardo.

"Ah Rick, that's tough. I'm sorry."

Ricardo waved it off.

"Yeah, well, it's fine. It's totally fine. I shouldn't have asked him to move in. We moved too fast. You've got to take these things as a lesson. And I learned my lesson, alright. I'm done with men. They're nothing but pigs. In fact, I'm done with all of them – androgynous, bears, butches, bicurious, closets, cross-dressers, leathers, otters, queens, twinks, wolfs, fluids, fairies, plain old fags and really, sexual deviants of any kind. From now on, I'm staying straight as an arrow. I'm going full-on straight white male. I'm going to find me a woman with wide hips, preferably with a father who's willing to trade up for a few goats, and I'm going to fornicate her repeatedly until her loins yield a satisfactory miniature replica of me. Then, and only then Mao, will I finally feel fulfilled!"

"Jesus Christ!"

Mao's response was involuntary. He was used to Ricardo's outrageous comments, but this one went beyond the pale.

"Don't use Jesus' name in vain, Mao. Besides, the jury is still out on how he feels about gays. We know from rednecks holding picket signs that God allegedly hates them, but as for Jesus... the jury is still out. For all we know, Jesus might have been gay himself."

Mao was bewildered at what he was hearing.

"Holy fuck, Rick, that's too far."

"But of course, there was no holy fuck. The conception was immaculate... everyone knows that."

Mao was shaking his head in disbelief.

"Ricardo, you're a real motherfucker, you know that?"

But Ricardo wasn't finished.

"Motherfucker? You talking about me, or Jesus? Because Jesus is technically God, and Mary is technically his mother, and God technically impregnated Mary... so technically Jesus is the original motherfucker. But then, I guess that means he isn't gay. But then again, what about me? I know plenty of guys who..."

Mao, his head on the verge of exploding, interjected.

"Okay, please, enough. I can literally feel myself getting dumber."

"But Mao, all I'm saying is..."

Mao put his hand up.

"I'm begging you, stop."

Ricardo opened his mouth, but then thought better of it. He sat quietly observing Mao with a wide, shit-eating grin on his face.

Mao, still wide-eyed, took a deep breath.

"Rick, I am trying to be a good friend here, and I am sorry about you and Keith, but you can't say that shit, man. It's 2019. If anyone ever hears you, your ass is going to get canceled faster than Cosby."

Ricardo perked up.

"Oh, Mao, you really are such a little drama queen. Besides, I can't get canceled, I'm on the spectrum."

Mao looked perplexed.

"The spectrum? You mean the autism spectrum?"

'That makes a lot of sense, actually,' Mao thought.

Ricardo shook his head earnestly.

"No, silly. I mean the LGBTQIA2S+BIPOC spectrum. It covers a wide array of different people from different backgrounds and of different sexual preferences, of all different walks of life; it's an umbrella term of inclusion that covers pretty much everyone... except for people like you."

Mao sighed. Of course that was Ricardo's reply.

"You are a terrible person."

Ricardo looked at Mao, and with a glimmer of mischief in his eyes, said:

"Everyone knows that there are absolutely no bad people on the spectrum. So, if anyone is getting canceled, or needs to watch what they say, it's you Mao."

Mao rolled his eyes.

"Alright, sure. You can't say I didn't warn you. When the time comes, you need to remember that I did what I could for you."

He took a breath, still shaking his head at Ricardo's stupid comments.

"Anyway, were you serious? Do you really think that having a kid would make you happy?"

Ricardo smirked.

"Well, Mr. Nosy, if you must know, I was only half-joking. I don't have too much extra time on my hands these days... But now, if you'll kindly exit the vehicle, it looks like there is, as usual, a line outside of *Pince,* and it is my professional opinion that the sooner we get into that line, the sooner we will be seated. The least you can do, seeing as I will no doubt be picking up the cheque here today, is to feed the meter. So, please make yourself useful."

Shaking his head, and wondering in barely audible mutterings why, despite all Ricardo's abrasive qualities and questionable views, he still regularly hung out with the idiot, Mao stepped out into the cold and like a good boy, did as he was told.

XXX

Fragments of Mao's Notes

09/01/2020

Lights. Screens. Ads. Distractions. Lights. Screens. Ads. **YOU.** *Distractions. Lights. Screens. Ads. Distractions. Lights. Screens. Ads. Distractions. Lights. Screens. Ads. Distractions. Lights. Screens. Ads. Distractions. Lights. Screens. Ads. Distractions.*

Lights. Screens. Ads. Distractions. Lights. **ARE.** *Screens. Ads. Distractions. Lights. Screens. Ads. Distractions. Lights. Screens. Ads. Distractions. Lights. Screens. Ads. Distractions. Lights. Screens. Ads. Distractions. Lights. Screens. Ads. Distractions. Lights. Screens. Ads. Distractions. Lights. Screens. Ads. Distractions. Lights. Screens. Ads. Distractions. Lights. Screens. Ads. Distractions. Lights. Screens. Ads. Distractions. Lights. Screens. Ads.*

Simulation. Stimulation. Entertainment Now. Simulation. Stimulation. Entertainment Now. Simulation. Stimulation. Entertainment Now. Simulation. Stimulation. Entertainment Now. Simulation. Stimulation. Entertainment Now. Simulation. Stimulation. Entertainment Now. Simulation. Stimulation. Entertainment Now. Simulation. Stimulation. Entertainment Now. Simulation. Stimulation. Entertainment Now. Simulation. Stimulation. Entertainment Now. Simulation. Stimulation. Entertainment Now. Simulation. **IN***. Stimulation. Entertainment Now. Simulation. Stimulation. Entertainment Now. Simulation. Stimulation. Entertainment Now. Simulation. Stimulation. Entertainment Now. Simulation. Stimulation. Entertainment Now. Simulation. Stimulation. Entertainment Now. Simulation. Stimulation. Entertainment Now. Simulation. Stimulation. Entertainment Now. Simulation. Stimulation. Entertainment Now. Simulation. Stimulation. Entertainment Now. Simulation. Stimulation. Entertainment Now. Simulation. Stimulation. Entertainment Now. Simulation. Stimulation. Entertainment Now. Simulation. Stimulation. Entertainment Now. Simulation. Stimulation. Entertainment Now. Simulation.*

Stimulation. Entertainment Now. Simulation. Stimulation. Entertainment Now. Simulation. Stimulation. Entertainment Now. **THERE**. *Simulation. Stimulation. Entertainment Now. Simulation. Stimulation. Entertainment Now. Simulation. Stimulation. Entertainment Now. Simulation. Stimulation. Entertainment Now. Simulation. Stimulation. Entertainment Now. Simulation. Stimulation. Entertainment Now. Simulation. Stimulation. Entertainment Now. Simulation. Stimulation. Entertainment Now. Simulation. Stimulation. Entertainment Now. Simulation. Stimulation. Entertainment Now. Simulation. Stimulation. Entertainment Now. Simulation. Stimulation. Entertainment Now. Simulation. Stimulation. Entertainment Now. Simulation. Stimulation. Entertainment Now. Simulation. Stimulation. Entertainment Now. Simulation. Stimulation. Entertainment Now. Simulation. Stimulation. Entertainment Now. Simulation. Stimulation. Entertainment Now. Simulation. Stimulation. Entertainment Now. Simulation.*

Contemplation. Information. Answers on the go. Always in the know. Contemplation. Information. Answers on the go. Always in the know. Contemplation. Information. Answers on the go. Always in the know. Contemplation. Information. Answers on the go. Always in the know. Contemplation. Information. Answers on the go. Always in the know. Contemplation. Information. Answers on the go. Always in the know. Contemplation. Information. Answers on the go. Always in the know. Contemplation. Information. Answers on the go. Always in the know. Contemplation. Information. Answers on the go. Always in the know. Contemplation. Information. Answers on the go. Always in the know. Contemplation. Information. Answers on the go. Always in the know. Contemplation. Information. **SOME.** *Answers on the go. Always in the know. Contemplation. Information. Answers on the go. Always in the know. Contemplation. Information. Answers on the go. Always in the know. Contemplation. Information. Answers on the go. Always in the know. Contemplation. Information. Answers on the go. Always in the know. Contemplation. Information. Answers on the go. Always in the know. Contemplation. Information. Answers on the go. Always in the know. Contemplation. Information. Answers on the go. Always in the know. Contemplation. Information. Answers on the go. Always in the know. Contemplation. Information. Answers on the go. Always in the know. Contemplation. Information. Answers on the go. Always in the* *know. Contemplation. Information. Answers on the go. Always in the know. Contemplation. Information. Answers on the go. Always in the know. Contemplation. Information. Answers on the go. Always in the know. Contemplation. Information. Answers on the go. Always in the know. Contemplation. Information. Answers on the go. Always in the know. Contemplation. Information. Answers on the go. Always in the know. Contemplation. Information. Answers on the go. Always in the know. Contemplation. Information. Answers on the go. Always in the know. Contemplation. Information. Answers on the go. Always in the know. Contemplation. Information. Answers on the go. Always in the know. Contemplation. Information. Answers on the go. Always in the know. Contemplation. Information.* **WHERE.** *Answers on the go. Always in the know. Contemplation. Information. Answers on the go. Always in the know. Contemplation. Information. Contemplation. Information. Answers on the go. Always in the know. Contemplation. Information. Answers on the go. Always in the know. Contemplation. Information. Answers on the go. Always in the know. Contemplation. Information. Answers on the go. Always in the know. Contemplation. Information. Answers on the go. Always in the know. Contemplation. Information. Answers on the go. Always in the know. Contemplation. Information. Answers on the go. Always in the know. Contemplation. Information. Answers on the go. Always in the know. Contemplation. Information.*

XXXI

Six days after the appointment had been set, Mao was seated on his sad excuse for a couch, mentally preparing himself for his journey across the hall.

Though outwardly Mao appeared calm and collected, inwardly, he was surprised by the fact that he felt... well, it's a little silly to say, but he felt rather nervous.

'Oh, come now, you're just experiencing nerves because this is something you've never done before!' he told himself. 'It's something new, something outside of your comfort zone. There isn't anything more to it than that,' he insisted unconvincingly. However, perceptive reader who always seems to be at least one step ahead, the truth was that the tension eating Mao up from the inside while he sat there on his shitty couch, well, it all arose from just one undeniable fact. And that one fact, sweet reader, was this: despite all the reasons he might have had to be skeptical, Mao wasn't really sure how he felt about the Mystic of Mimijad. On the one hand, the whole persona was obviously a big crock. Balderdash. Poppycock! Complete nonsense, naturally. Naturally! That would be any sane person's appraisal of the situation *at face value*. Although, on the other hand, one might shrewdly point out that Mao wasn't exactly any sane person.

Mao, excellent reader, was an *artist*.

What we mean to express through that italicized detail is simply that artists often have a special softness for these kinds of things. Artists, you see, are *meant* to let some of that strangeness, some of that *bizarreness* floating around out there in the ether, they are meant to let it permeate the vacuum seal so many mortals try to create between their little worlds and the grand unknown that invariably lies beyond. Magic, mysticism, myth, superstition, religion, occultism – really any and all conjectures about the nature of the unknown, no matter how outlandish these could sometimes seem *at face value* – these are the creative's bread and butter. Meat and potatoes. Beetroot and beetroot. You see what we are saying? Without any of these supernatural, or metaphysical conjectures, all an artist would be left with was dry, cold, uninteresting facts. Or, philosophically speaking, all he would be left with was *dry, cold, uninteresting rationalism.* Yes, that's it. All you have left when you strip away the magic, the mystery of things is dry, cold rationalism.

What a bore!

Mao didn't want to admit it to himself, but it was undeniable in the pit of his stomach: he felt that special tingle of excitement reserved for someone just about to step firmly into the unknown. Firmly, indeed. For to step falteringly into the unknown is to move in fear. But that was not it. That was not it at all. Mao felt no fear. He felt no apprehension. He knew the feeling quite well, and in spite of his unwillingness to acknowledge it, the feeling had a name. And that name, beautiful reader, was *excitement.* But why wouldn't Mao admit to himself that he felt excited? Well, the reason for that, too, was very simple: for Mao to admit his excitement would be to admit to the legitimacy of the lunatic across the hall. Or, at the very least, to admit excitement at the prospect of hearing the mad ravings of the lunatic across the hall would be to admit to the existence of some flaw within himself, which he hoped to remedy through a moment of epiphany triggered by the mad ravings and slapdash auspices of the very same lunatic across the hall!

Either way he sliced it, both propositions were *precarious,* to say the least.

Speaking with the Mystic of Mimijad about anything of substance would be well outside of Mao's comfort zone. There was no doubt about that. Mao rarely spoke to strangers, and even more rarely did he speak to them about his innermost desires. What's more is that, in spite of it all, poetic graces and delusions of grandeur duly considered, Mao still considered himself a rational man! He didn't believe in ghosts, or spirits, or omens... well, alright, maybe he did believe in omens. Yes, we've confirmed already that he did indeed believe in omens. But that, again, was only because he was a literary man! That last one is forgivable. What is an artist without his quirks?

But if people somehow found out he had visited a mystic... *ouf.*

That was something else entirely.

They'd think he'd gone straight off the deep end.

But then, maybe he *had* gone off the deep end. He *was* going a little mad these last few months, caught in the grips of grieving his failed relationship, and deprived of his usual reprieve of writing honestly about his emotions, and so purging himself of them. Then again, he had been trying so fantastically hard! Because of that effort, and the way that he desperately scoured the world around him for a lead, an idea, a notion that might sprout into something, anything of merit, the way that he looked at everything not as hard and real, but instead as a potential portal into the fanciful flight of his imagination, because of this, this, this figurative interpretation of the world, he often asked himself in moments of solitude and reticence: what is genuine, and what is contrived in the hopes of creating a compelling narrative? In the murky waters of Mao's overtaxed psyche, the distinction was no longer clear, it seemed. What was even worse, reader, was that if it *was* true that his real life had become his canvas, and that his life had degenerated into nothing more than a *narrative* he was *contriving* for the sake of his craft, then wasn't it just utterly *tragic* that the *narrative* he was *crafting* was not even in the least bit *compelling?*

Let's not answer that question.

Suffice it to say, Mao felt like a man in a cage, and the cage, vexatiously, was built of the familiar, though detrimentally self-serving neural pathways boxing him into his own cozy, familiar mind. Routine, reader! Grooves on a smooth vinyl surface. He thought about A-Z every single day still, though he hadn't heard even a peep from her. She was most probably still out there in orbit, floating around somewhere in the vast, wide world, more than likely living it up and enjoying her life. And here he was sulking, uninspired, and miserable! Inhabiting a body moving in the present, shackled to a mind caught in the snare of the past.

Reader, we don't know of a worse affliction in this world.

To account for things that need accounting for, graceful, delicate, and shockingly intelligent reader, we feel impelled to acknowledge that, yes, it was part of Mao's original plan to feel 'miserable'. However! Ah, the big H word! However! What was absolutely not part of the plan, sensitive and charitable reader, was *actually* feeling miserable! Mao was supposed to feel 'miserable' in the way that rock stars and other speed living advocates were 'miserable': only in theory, because their long train of ephemeral, superficial pleasures always moved quick enough to stave off the cumbersome reality of negative emotions forever trailing behind. That is, of course, until the train ran out of steam, reality quickly caught up, the passengers got walloped by karma's boomerang, and in the throes of their pain they managed to produce the moving piece of art lurking within that was always going to justify the whole ordeal!

No, regrettably, it didn't seem to be panning out that way for Mao. The poor bastard wasn't even sleeping with any groupies, in spite of the uptake in drugs we might add, and he wasn't writing anything even coherent, never mind anything that could be potentially considered generational and/or timeless and/or moving. All he could muster, still, were those disjointed, rambling shards of irrelevance that took the form of loopy rants, or of false starts upon the leisurely promenade to profundity. And these, we don't need to tell you, have *zero* commercial value, and so, are absolutely *useless.*

Maybe that's why he felt that tingle of excitement. Maybe, deep down, Mao hoped that the Mystic of Mimijad, or J.C., or whatever his name was could actually help him. Maybe Mao had finally reached his breaking point, and was ready to admit that he needed help. He was in a lousy place, mentally and emotionally, and at the moment, there was only one person who was offering to help him find a way out of it. Granted, that person was somewhere on the spectrum between a little nutty and institutionally insane, but hey, at the very least the guy seemed to be in good spirits most of the time. The loon across the hall was not a doctor, not in any real sense of the word (except maybe 'quack'), but he *was* a human being. As such, there was at least a slight chance he could offer some insight. He was older than Mao, too, and he was foreign. He was confident. He was *really* confident. He had to be, to pull off that wardrobe. He had some things going for him.

Maybe he could offer Mao some ancient Mimijadian wisdom? Recite some Mimijadian proverbs? Sing songs of love and devotion to the Mimijadian muses?

Who knows?

Maybe, just maybe, if Mao managed not to be so cynical about it, he could find something of value and meaning in his encounter with the Mystic of Mimijad. And reader, let's be honest, that's obviously what he was hoping for. Although, that hope was tucked away somewhere way deeper than the superficial concerns of his neocortex.

Indeed, reader, the place where hope lies in wait is always somewhere darker, and more remote than the superficial concerns of one's neocortex.

Anyhow, despite his concerns about looking silly, Mao did make sure to adhere to the Mystic of Mimijad's preliminary requirements. If for no other reason, at least the madman wouldn't have anything to harangue him about. If the charm was going to fall flat, or if the magical force field was going to fizzle out, or whatever, it wasn't going to be because Mao hadn't followed proper protocol. And so, Mao washed his body with the uncomfortably viscous liquid he had been given. Even more importantly, he completely ignored the fact that the thick liquid smelled a little (a lot) like Aunt Jemima. In fact, Mao made a point *not* to taste it. Whether it was Aunt Jemima or not was entirely beside the point. Placebo pills only work when you don't ask too many questions. Furthermore, judicious reader, Mao had adhered to the mystic's command to abstain from any sexual activity for the forty-eight hours leading up to their rendezvous. And that, as you can imagine, was tough! Those two days were some of the longest of his life, as Mao was deprived of one of his absolute favorite alone time activities.

And then, finally, the time came.

There on his dilapidated couch, Mao glanced at his watch and noticed it was seven fifty-five. His appointment with the mystic was set for eight. He would, of course, be punctual.

Mao got up and stood before the mirror by the front door, taking in what he saw. His clothes were clean, and his long, bushy beard was tidy. His eyes felt sharp as he peered into them through the glass. One had to gaze a little deeper into his reflection, though, to notice something was off. The irises of his soft, feminine eyes, which were usually of a strikingly deep brown, struck him that night as somehow hollow. As he studied the reflection staring back at him through the lens, the eyes seemed unreal to him, and fragile, like the deep brown irises had been swapped for cheap, thin strips of foil. Suddenly, his self-awareness grew overly acute, as he stood there swallowing his reflection in the glass. It seemed vulgar to him that he should stare at himself like that. It seemed self-indulgent. Or worse, *self-annihilating*. The thought occurred to him that he was staring at some sort of contemptuous meat puppet, dangling by the strings of fortune. As he analyzed, he almost managed to forget that *he* was the puppet. Then, it felt too weird being aware of the strings. He looked away. Though, he did retain the presence of mind to reach for his smartphone, and jot a few notes down.

He stepped into the bathroom to comb his beard one last time, and applied a little cologne to mask the pervasive scent of high fructose corn syrup that seemed to have penetrated beneath his epidermis. As he walked to the front door, he noticed the door of his spare room was open again. 'Who keeps opening that bloody door,' he wondered as he peered in, acknowledging the two bags of his ex-lover's things still lingering in the cluttered space where his work desk (that hadn't seen any work for the longest) remained in perpetual disarray. Promising to deal with that later, he slammed the door firmly shut. He put on the white tennis sneakers he always wore, and unlocked the heavy chain locked door to his Apartment #7.

Lucky #7.

That's what he thought when he first visited the apartment. It was a numerological omen that denoted a driving desire for spiritual wisdom and knowledge. It dictated that his tenure would be one of exceeding good fortune.

Had it been?

On the threshold of the world beyond his bubble, Mao took a deep breath. He looked across the checkered tiles and yellowing walls of the hall to the door across the way: Apartment #8.

Magic #8.

A numerological omen of balance, and harmony.

But then, perhaps this was reading too much into things.

Mao locked his door and strode across the hall to the door of the infamous Apartment #8. Though the distance traveled was a mere seven or eight strides of his muscular, vital legs, each measured step felt elongated, as though charged with ineffable importance. There seemed, tonight, right there in the hall, a special radiance in the air.

It wasn't that any single detail he observed stood out to him. No, it was instead some inexpressible feeling that, if only for tonight, all of the details converging to create his happenstance perspective seemed to be in perfect agreement. He felt, walking over to the magic Apartment #8, that he was exactly where he was meant to be.

But then perhaps, dear reader, this was reading too much into things.

He lifted his arm and rapped his knuckles on the door three times.

Knock, knock, knock.

Hardly had the third knock been knocked but the door swung open, revealing the Mystic of Mimijad in the doorway, resplendent in full, glorious regalia. The flowing fuchsia habit seemed to have been cleanly pressed for the occasion, as did the floppy white hat. The dark Malacca cane dangling from his right hand was ominous as ever, and the gold jackal perched atop seemed to smile in the yellow light of the hall. However, despite all there was to be impressed with, the only thing that occurred to Mao, taking in his neighbor, was the irrepressible fact that the man didn't ever seem to change his clothes, or swap out his props.

(For the sake of clarity, esteemed reader, Jajùmissu Cá *did* change his clothes. He did so every day, in fact. The man had eight identical habits, one labeled for each day of the week, as per Mimijadian custom, and even one extra to account for potential laundering emergencies. As for the Malacca cane, well, that, unfortunately, was his only one. When working out the final details for what would become the Mystic of Mimijad's signature look, the measured and calculated Cá did his share of research on mystical accoutrements, and decided, not without due consideration, that he would be better off investing in one really good, solid, vaguely magical walking stick, which would provide the genuine mystical airs he was after, and also, thanks to its excellent twentieth century craftsmanship, last for a very long time, rather than purchasing the cheap array of interchangeable, frivolous, China-made accessories advocated by twenty-first century consumerism. For that reason, he only had that one cane, or 'prop', as Mao somewhat cynically put it. Though, we really think the one was enough, as it was a mightily magnificent cane, a one of a kind piece almost perfectly accommodating our beloved mystic's generous dimensions and eccentric sartorial tastes).

In addition to his flowing fuchsia robes, Mao noticed the Mystic of Mimijad had donned the infamous black-and-white beads he reserved for his consultations with 'patients'. He was also effusing his characteristically sterile odor. Upon performing his own quick inward analysis of Mao's unremarkable t-shirt and jeans appearance, the mystic's face took on an air of solemnity. He raised his chin and frowned very seriously, looking Mao up and down as though appraising a used car that's been sitting on a lot for too long, or an old kitchen appliance that's been marked down three or four times, before low-balling the salesman for the absolute best price, without even the slightest of qualms about walking away from anything other than a promptly accepted offer. J.C. even had to check his impulse to kick Mao, just to make sure he wouldn't fall apart.

"Miboy."

The mystic's voice was deep and grave.

"The Mystic of Mimijad is ready to see you. But before you enter his *atelier*, he must be sure that you followed instructions. You did what I told you to do, yes?"

He? I? The jumbled perspectives, and really the absurdity of the whole situation left Mao feeling a little mixed up.

"Yes, of course. I did everything he, I mean you asked."

"Everything?" the mystic's voice boomed.

"Everything, O great one!"

Mao put his palms together and bowed. Jajùmissu Cá's eyes narrowed.

"You washed your body with the curse-cleansing concoction I graciously provided, free of charge, yes?"

Mao coughed, suppressed a smile.

"Oh, uh, yes. I, uh, lathered every nook and cranny of my body with the Aunt Je-, uh, I mean the curse-cleanser. Though, I do have to admit I was a little concerned about the vivid hallucinations I experienced. Are those normal, wise one?"

Jajùmissu Cá looked Mao over ever more suspiciously.

"What kind of hallucinations, miboy?"

Mao didn't miss a beat.

"Every time I closed my eyes, O great one, I saw legions of strange, humanoid pancake creatures carrying swords and galloping towards me on horseback..."

J.C. wasn't quite sure whether the kid was really that gullible, or if he was being mocked. The Mystic of Mimijad, however, was a professional. He knew better than to get sidetracked by any silliness he himself had not contrived. He cut Mao off.

"Indeed. That is a common side effect, and you need not worry, miboy. The visions simply confirm that the powerful concoction is working. Still, the Mystic of Mimijad must be sure. Young man, come here and let me smell you."

Mao hesitated, but the mystic was definitely serious. Mao leaned forward, and the Mystic of Mimijad yanked Mao's arm and brought it up to his nose, sniffing it like a hungry, probing anteater.

"Mhm, yes, mhm. Good. The Mystic of Mimijad is satisfied!"

The mystic rubbed his nose and sniffed frantically, leaving Mao wondering if he might have been jamming something up there before opening the door. Suddenly, the mystic leaned in and whispered conspiratorially.

"And you did not... how shall I say, *pet the cat,* correct?"

The Mystic of Mimijad arched an eyebrow meaningfully. Mao looked up at him blankly.

"I don't remember you saying anything about cats, but I don't have one, so no. There are no animals allowed in the building, you know. There's a pretty clear sign listing all the building rules in the lobby."

The Mystic of Mimijad straightened up and shook his head earnestly.

"No, no, young man. Don't be silly. I know there are no animals allowed in the building. The cat I referred to was *metaphorical.* You know... you didn't *shake the milkman's hand* since we spoke last, did you miboy?"

Mao was perplexed. This was Montréal in early 2020. Mao wasn't old enough to have ever seen a milkman. The Mystic of Mimijad sighed.

"You didn't *polish the banister* lad, or go into *manual override?*"

'Lad? That's a first,' Mao noted.

"Look, I just did what you said to do. And I was kidding about the humanoid pancake creatures. I hardly did anything today. Just some light reading."

The Mystic of Mimijad began to get a little frustrated.

"Yes, that's just what I mean! You didn't *cook the cucumber,* or *beat the one-eyed boxer?* You know, you didn't *give yourself a hand,* or *celebrate Palm Sunday,* did you, young man? Because it's very important that you didn't! It would jeopardize the integrity of our entire rendezvous!"

The mystic was blinking his eyes wildly. Mao wasn't sure if he was trying to convey something in Morse code, or if he was suffering from an aneurysm. Either way, Mao didn't understand what he was getting so animated about. He shrugged.

"I'm not religious. Besides, isn't Palm Sunday in the springtime?"

"Ugh!"

The Mystic of Mimijad sighed and leaned forward on his Malacca cane. He waved his free arm emphatically.

"You're not understanding, miboy. What I mean to ask is, you didn't *choke the chicken,* or *chase the majestic white tiger out of its dark, spherical lair* did you?"

Mao was at a loss.

"I already told you I don't have any animals. It's against building rules. Although that last thing you just said was really specific. Do you really have white tigers back in Mimijad?"

Jajùmissu Cá dragged his palm the length of his face as he rolled his eyes. He grumbled under his breath:

"You didn't *masturbate* in the last forty-eight hours, did you?"

"Oh! Why didn't you just say so? My *goodness* that was a painfully long way round! Where in the world did you even learn all those euphemisms? Do Mimijadians have some sort of complex about the word 'masturbate'? No. I didn't *masturbate* in the last forty-eight hours. For heaven's *sake,* sir."

Jajùmissu Cá leaned on his Malacca cane and stared at Mao sardonically. He just about retorted, but remembered himself in the nick of time. It wasn't worth it. J.C. snapped back into character as he slammed his walking stick down on the tiled floor of the hall.

"Silence!"

Mao jumped back in surprise. The mystic widened his eyes menacingly at Mao for a moment before relaxing them. The performance had the desired effect.

"Good. It is important that you did not do that in the last forty-eight hours. It would break the seal of purity required to properly access the deepest recesses of your mind, miboy. The Mystic of Mimijad is pleased. Now, please come in."

The Mystic of Mimijad bowed gallantly, welcoming Mao into his sanctum. Mao stepped into the apartment, penetrating its field of energy for the first time. Though the ever-present smell of boxed macaroni and cheese lingered, it was little more than an accent to the prominent, delightful aroma of patchouli whirling up from the sticks of burning incense on the mystic's large wooden chest. Mao navigated his way carefully into the room, mindful of each step across the rugs littered with burning candles. Any other light that might have entered the apartment was completely obscured by the thick drawn curtains. Although, the confluence of dancing flames did create an ample glow, shining upon the blank faces of the ceramic idols and the silver cross still propped up by the inexplicably Christian taxidermy squirrel.

The mystic closed the door softly behind him, then came around to escort Mao through the candles, and around the tripod pointed at the red velvet chesterfield. He led Mao over to a black, raggedy-looking folding chair placed at the back of the room, by the broken TV monitor still struggling to find reception. The Mystic of Mimijad seated himself with folded legs on one of the rugs beside the smooth, white plastic surface Mao had noticed the first time he peered into the enchanted hovel. Beside the mystic lay a big, open, leather-bound book revealing the strange alphabet of a language Mao had never seen before. Scattered about were dozens of loose papers scrawled upon in the mystic's handwriting. At an arm's reach, the sinister candelabra effused its gothic blue glow. Within the radius of its distinctly haunting light sat seven polished shells, as well as the plush conch still full to bursting with colorful Canadian tender.

Everything seemed to be as Mao remembered seeing it, except for one crucial detail. As he scanned the room, Mao could not locate the plate of onions, peppers and lemons that had fascinated him the last time he stole a glance into the mystic's *atelier.*

"Hey, mister, what happened to the plate with the onions?"

The Mystic of Mimijad had his head down, sorting the paraphernalia required for today's charlatanic ritual.

"Onions?"

The question was asked in a neutral, uninterested tone.

"Yeah, the last time I got a good look into your place, I noticed a plate of sliced onions, peppers, and lemons on the floor, with four teacup candles on top in a perfect rhombus formation. I don't see it this time. What happened to it?"

Jajùmissu Cá looked at Mao like he was crazy, and was about to tell him as much before he caught himself again. 'This kid is messing with me, trying to get me to break character. But, I won't let him. I am a professional, and I will win this battle of attrition. By the end of this, he will be eating out of my hand. For I am The Mystic of Mimijad!'

These were the types of things that went on in J.C.'s head. He was really quite good at pepping himself up.

The Mystic of Mimijad looked over very seriously at Mao.

"I have no idea what you are talking about, miboy."

Mao's eyebrows shot up in shock. 'Is this guy lying to me? There's treachery afoot, and it's got something to do with that plate of onions! By George, I'll stake my reputation as a detective on it!'

Mao's mind was racing, and he was working himself into indignation. He tried to get a hold of himself. He was clearly overreacting. It was just a plate of onions.

"Oh, okay. Well, never mind, then."

The two locked eyes for a moment. The tension was palpable. They were like two heavyweight fighters feeling each other out, probing for any sign of fear.

The mystic spoke first, reassuming his role as ringmaster.

"Now, if you would, please hush. I must prepare my things."

The mystic focused on his book, and shuffled a few papers around. He mumbled unintelligibly to himself as Mao turned around, returning to his admiration of the oddities scattered about the apartment. There was plenty else to fascinate him besides the mysterious plate of onions.

As he looked around, Mao couldn't help but notice that the folding chair he was sitting on kept squeaking. *Squeak. Squeak.* The damn thing squeaked with his every twist and turn! After about a dozen squeaks, Mao had had enough. 'This guy leaves a conch shell full of cash out in the open, but makes me sit on a decrepit squeaking folding chair. Unbelievable. I oughta say something. No, c'mon Mao, just let it go. No, no, I oughta say something. I'm the customer, and the customer is always right,' he thought, as he fired himself into a state of righteous indignation. This was something Mao did quite a lot.

"Hey, hi, hey, so sorry to interrupt again, but you wouldn't happen to have some WD-40 lying around, would you?"

The mystic looked up from his papers, doing his best not to get aggravated. He was fully concentrated on the task at hand, and inwardly chastising himself for his lack of organization. The chaos of scattered papers left a better impression on his patients, sure, but his life would be so much easier if he just got himself a binder, or a duo tang. It would also probably keep him a little further than one false step away from burning the entire building down every day. J.C. was searching through the scattered papers for a particular document labeled 'Mimijadian Shell Reading for Dummies', which laid out the procedure in simple, step-by-step directions, and with illustrations. He always kept this printout handy, as a cheat sheet, and incorporated it into the act to make sure he didn't forget anything. Besides, it wasn't like anyone in Canada had ever laid eyes on the Mimijadian alphabet. The mystic realized this in one of his first consultations, making mental note of the way the Mimijadian figures mystified his patients. Since then, he made a point of leaving some documents or books out whenever he had a consultation, and even kept some laying by him on the couch when he made his YouTube videos. It was good for business. The leather-bound book, which the mystic had noticed Mao staring at (Mao had presumed it was a medieval book of spells), was actually just the standard issue Mimijadian Zoo Employee Manual.

"What?"

"WD-40. It's a lubricant. This chair is *very* squeaky."

Jajùmissu Cá snorted angrily and balled his fists. This kid was really getting on his nerves. 'How dare he insult me in my own home?' the Mimijadian thought. He was capable of firing himself up, too. However, he composed himself in time. It was the Mystic of Mimijad's job to have the answer to everything. Even a squeaky chair.

J.C. took a deep breath.

"That is a very special chair, young man. It is meant to squeak. The squeak is indicative of positive frequencies being emitted into the room. I have all my patients sit on that chair, miboy. If it does not squeak, I know immediately that I cannot work with them. The squeak is good. In fact, the squeak is not only good, it is integral to how we do things here, lad. No squeak would be a great cause for concern. We need the squeak."

Mao looked at him skeptically, but seemed to grant that the mystic's spiel was yet a passable answer. Mao nodded, and the Mystic of Mimijad returned to his preparations. Mao began to look around again, mulling it over. He wanted to maintain the good frequencies, sure, but that squeak! It was unbearable! Finally, he decided he couldn't quite swallow it.

"Look, I get all that about the frequencies, but I'm really sorry, I don't think I'm going to be able to handle this squeak. Is there really nothing you can do? I can't be the first one to complain about this chair."

The mystic looked at him with glazed eyes, and replied flatly.

"You can join me on the floor, if you prefer."

Mao felt that was reasonable. He sat himself in a folded position across from the mystic. Mao had never been this close to the mystic before, and the proximity was quite rousing. He was sure he could feel the man's aura. As though sensing his thoughts, the mystic looked up from his papers and into Mao's curious eyes. Up close, Mao noticed the mystic's immaculately pedicured toenails. From his vantage point, J.C. decided Mao's nose hairs could use a trim.

"Okay, miboy, the Mystic of Mimijad is ready."

The mystic hadn't found the document he was looking for, but felt confident he could get by. He'd done this dozens of times, after all. It would be like muscle memory. Besides, the sooner they started, the sooner he could get this imbecile out of his apartment.

The mystic reached into the folds of his fuchsia robes and fished out a smartphone. He put some deep, tonal, ambient music on, and then returned the phone from whence it came. Then, he took hold of the plush conch shell. This, he raised above his head with both hands, causing some of the money inside to cascade down onto him. He began to emit loud, guttural sounds, with his eyes closed and the veins on his temple throbbing.

After over a minute of this, Mao was on the verge of bursting into laughter when Jajùmissu Cá suddenly stopped, and gently put the shell down. He opened his eyes and looked at Mao peacefully.

"You brought the money, yes?"

"Yeah, but I kinda wanted to hold on to this cash. Do you take cards or e-transfer?"

The mystic stared at Mao and blinked three times. It took every ounce of his professional composure not to throw Mao out the door. He had to give it to the kid, no one had ever asked him that question before. J.C. looked at the conch shell, and then slowly back at Mao. Then back at the conch shell, and back at Mao. Mao followed his eyes, waiting patiently for an answer to his question. The mystic's expression softened, as he let out a sigh. He was slowly realizing this session was going to be harder than he thought.

"No, miboy. The Mystic of Mimijad does not accept cards or e-transfer."

"Oh, alright then."

Mao reached into his pocket for his wallet and produced the twenty-dollar bill. The sight of the cold, hard cash did the flailing mystic some good.

"Okay, very good. You see those shells on the floor by your foot, miboy? Yes, those. Take them and wrap the money around them. Yes, like that. Now, squeeze very tight. Very, very tight. Yes! Good. Now, visualize what you want most in this world. Don't tell me yet, just visualize. And squeeze it tight, tight, tight. Good, miboy. Now, give me the twenty dollars."

Mao did as he was told. The Mystic of Mimijad took the bill, held it up with both hands as if in sacrifice to some perverse god, lingered in that ridiculous pose for a few seconds, and then promptly stuffed the cash into the plush conch shell and tucked it away out of sight.

"Good, miboy. The seal is confirmed. Our work can begin."

Both men exhaled in relief.

"I will begin by asking you a series of questions, which you will answer honestly. Do you agree?"

Mao nodded.

Like a deft magician, the mystic reached into another hidden compartment of his habit and produced a green marker. Mao wondered what other tricks the mystic had hidden up the folds of his flowing fuchsia robes, but he dropped the thought quickly as the mystic's eyes bore into him like a drill. The marker was poised beside a blank sheet of paper, which the mystic leaned against the leather-bound book to create a suitable writing surface.

"Let's start with your name."

"Mao."

The Mystic of Mimijad blew on the tip of the marker like he meant to eat it, but it was still too hot. Then, he put the tip of the marker to his ear, and nodded vigorously. Then, he sputtered onto the tip of the marker, as though he were spitting out sunflower seeds. Then, he wrote something unintelligible on the piece of paper. Mao leaned over to take a look. It seemed to him like just your run-of-the-mill, household squiggly line. The mystic's enthusiasm swept him back into the moment.

"Good. Good. And tell me, miboy, why have you come to seek the counsel of the Mystic of Mimijad?"

The mystic raised an eyebrow, and tilted his head back, making a face like some demented wizard about to cast a spell. Mao cleared his throat. He knew this question would come. He had wondered what he would say when it inevitably did. He had considered fabricating a story, but then, that seemed to him like so much more work than merely telling the truth. Besides, it wasn't as though this man could somehow hurt him if Mao told the truth. The Mystic of Mimijad, in all likelihood, couldn't care less about Mao's petty troubles. All of this was perfunctory. It was like the first few questions the doctor would ask you, whenever you went in for a checkup. As if how many cigarettes you smoked per week had anything to do with your toe fungus... Mao thought that was a funny analogy, though, considering he was currently the Mystic of Mimijad's 'patient'. He had given the mystic the money, and now the mystic was going through the motions. He could 'protect' himself by abstracting himself from the truth through fiction, or in other words, lying, but where had that gotten him? He had been doing that for the past few months, attempting to sublimate his pain through storytelling, and had managed only to produce an awful almost-story riddled with pain. Everything would be easier if he simply told the truth. To do the same thing over and over again, and to expect different results, why, we all know where that leads...

Mao sighed.

"Alright. To be perfectly honest, I'm here because I've been feeling a little lost lately, mystic. I got my heart broken a few months ago, and the whole thing may have been entirely my fault. The healing process has been slow and arduous. I still think about her every day. What's more, I am a writer. I wrote a couple books, and they are doing okay. But lately, I've been trying to write again, a great, monumental novel about the postmodern condition, but I've found that the process is not quite as easy, or as enjoyable as it was the last two times. For the first time in my career, I am experiencing what I can only describe as absolutely crippling writer's block."

'Ah, a writer. I should have known. That explains *a lot*,' Jajùmissu Cá thought.

The Mystic of Mimijad looked at Mao sympathetically. He was surprised that the young man was speaking so candidly. In the brief time he had known Mao, Jajùmissu Cá had developed an impression of the young man as a very coiled, tightly-wound individual. It was almost touching to see him finally opening up. The young man had been so reluctant to share anything that might make him seem human, that this first genuinely vulnerable moment almost moved Jajùmissu Cá to tears. *Almost.* Tears were absolutely beyond the realm of the Mystic of Mimijad's stoic persona. The mystic kept it tight. Although, he did admittedly feel more inspired to do what he could to actually help the young man.

"Ah, heartbreak. She is a cruel mistress, and one can easily become addicted to her mistreatment. I knew it. I could tell by the look in your face. You bear the look of longing, miboy. Tell me, what is the person's name? It is a girl?"

Mao put his hands on his knees. It felt strange talking about his most vulnerable secrets with this stranger. On the other hand, something about the mystic and his queerness made Mao feel at ease. It was almost like he needed to talk to someone even crazier than he was, so that he could be sure he wouldn't be judged. Or, perhaps that was merely his neurotic impulse to rationalize the simple truth that sharing everything he had kept locked away for so long felt good.

"Yes. It was a girl. I mean, it *is* a girl. She isn't dead. Her name is A-Z."

The mystic whispered frantically to his marker. He listened for its answer, before adding more unintelligible symbols to the paper.

"A–Z, very good. And tell me, what is your date of birth?"

Mao told him.

"And do you know hers?"

Again, Mao told him. The mystic returned to his private dialogue with the marker, writing out more strange symbols.

The Mystic of Mimijad proceeded to ask some more basic questions: where they met, how old they were, what their favorite colors were. Then, just as Mao told him his favorite color was blue, the Mystic of Mimijad began to shake his head furiously and point excitedly at the unintelligible marks on the paper.

"Do you see? Young man! Based on what you have told me, yes... I am very sorry, but I must tell you the truth! The outlook is bad. Very bad! Then again, wait a minute, yes, yes! Oh, oh, yes! There it is! Do you see?"

Mao leaned forward to examine the paper. The madman was pointing furiously at a place where two of the squiggly lines he had drawn triumphantly converged.

"Do you see? Yes! There it is! It is a sign of happiness in your future. Yes! It is there, miboy! There is happiness. I see it! I see a lot of happiness. So much happiness! But... oh. I also see a lot of pain. Yes, it is so. The pain must come first, before the happiness. It is always so. But, I do believe you can make it through the storm... with my help, that is, miboy."

Mao frowned and readjusted his position on the floor as the mystic laughed maniacally and cast the papers aside.

"You said something about writer's block. Tell me a little bit about that."

Suddenly, he grabbed Mao firmly by the wrist, and began to slap his inner arm.

"Hey! Ow!"

The mystic paid no mind to Mao's complaints, but instead closed his eyes, maintaining his grip on Mao's wrist. Mao tried to yank his hand away, but the grip was tight. So, he took a deep breath, and yielded.

"Well, I've been writing for the past five or six years, and I've never run into an impediment like this. It's like every time I try to sit down and work, every fiber of my being just revolts against it. Like I said, I've been trying to put together a new novel, a satire, of sorts, but all I've been able to come up with are these disjointed bits and pieces that don't seem to fit together in any way. It doesn't feel authentic. I can't find any cohesion between the haphazard parts. I can't manage to create the harmony I'm looking for. I can't seem to find the missing ingredient."

The mystic nodded, and opened his eyes. He released Mao's arm and clapped his hands together. Then, he began fiddling convulsively with the beads around his neck.

"That is a very, very grave problem, miboy. Tell the Mystic of Mimijad, why do you think that is?"

'I am officially the acting guinea pig for the world's most perverse psychotherapy session' Mao thought. 'If I knew why that was, genius, I wouldn't be talking to you, now would I, Sigmund *Fraud?*' Mao's cynicism fed his rising anger. But then, he caught himself in the act. Maybe this head case was actually onto something. Just the little bit he managed to express before had made him feel better. Maybe just talking about it might actually help. At the very least, it would push him to put what he felt into words. Wasn't that exactly what he was after? Mao didn't want to get sidetracked by cynicism. It was too easy. It was the coward's way out. No, he wouldn't get sidetracked by cynicism. Not this time. Saying all of this out loud was good. Put it into words! What a revelation! He had to keep going. He might actually realize something he hadn't before.

"I'm not quite sure, mystic. That's the perfectly honest truth. I think it must have something to do with feeling heartbroken. At first, I thought I was happy with her, you know? I felt like things were going great. But then, the time passed and I noticed I wasn't writing. And I just got fixated on that. It made me feel miserable, in a sense. Can you understand that? I'm a writer. I need to write! Well, anyhow, I didn't understand it, and all I could think of was that I couldn't write because I was too happy. Or, maybe not happy, but satisfied. Sated. Maybe this won't make any sense to you, but I thought that I needed to be uncomfortable, in pain to write something beautiful. I felt like that was the way all the great ones did it. But, I couldn't bring myself to leave her. I loved her. Or, I thought I did. So, I sabotaged. I sabotaged until she had no choice but to do the dirty work for me. I lost her. But then, I thought that everything would be fine, because I would finally be able to write without her in the way, you know? I was in pain, and I was ready to channel that pain into beautiful writing. But that didn't happen. It's been months, and I still miss her, and I still haven't been able to write a thing. I... I just don't know what to make of it."

Though he didn't show it, Jajùmissu Cá was bewildered.

'Damn, I did not expect that. This young man most certainly has issues beyond the scope of my abilities. I should have just focused on selling him some crystals to bring the girl back,' he thought to himself. Nevertheless, the Mystic of Mimijad, always the consummate professional, managed to take things in stride.

"That is good. We have a lot of work to do, miboy. Let us consult the shells, and see what they can tell us."

The mystic picked up the seven shells, shook them gently, and scattered them upon the white plastic mat. He analyzed the spread carefully.

"Hmm. I see. Tell me, young man, are you active?"

Mao nodded eagerly. He was so swept away by the high of finally bringing his insecurities out into the open that he managed to willfully forget the fact that he was wearing a t-shirt, and that in that t-shirt, a heavily drugged and blind in one eye street urchin would have picked up on the fact that he probably worked out from time to time.

"Wow, how did you know that? Yes, I am pretty active."

The mystic pointed at one of the shells, which had landed a little further away from the others, which were more or less bunched together.

"Ah, I knew it! See?"

The Mystic of Mimijad folded his arms triumphantly as Mao inspected the shells. Then, the mystic promptly scooped them up again, and scattered them once more. Upon analysis of this latest spread, he narrowed his eyes and ventured:

"And tell me, miboy, this girl. She and you had much in common, yes?"

Mao nodded eagerly.

"Yes, yes, we did!"

"Ah, I knew it. See?"

The Mystic of Mimijad again folded his arms triumphantly, after pointing at a cluster of three shells. Mao's eyes widened in awe. The mystic threw the shells again.

"And tell me, miboy, you write. You hope to be famous someday, yes?"

Mao nodded eagerly.

"Oh, yes, yes, I do!"

"Ah, I knew it. See?"

The mystic pointed decisively at a place on the white mat where no shells had landed. Mao nodded even more eagerly than before. The mention of fame had captured his attention.

"Mystic of Mimijad, I must ask you, do you think I will be famous one day? Everyone knows I work really hard on my craft, and I know that fame should never be the goal, but I want it so much. Do you think I have what it takes?"

Jajùmissu Cá looked into the eyes of his mark and realized immediately how earnest Mao's question was. He had succeeded. As predicted, J.C. had Mao in the palm of his hand. In the mystic, medium, or diviner's line of work, this was the stuff of wet dreams. A mark hungry for your guidance, and hanging on your every word. What more could Jajùmissu Cá ask for? But then, something wasn't right. For the first time in his short, but illustrious career, the Mystic of Mimijad did not feel that bloodthirsty killer instinct needed to make it in the world of hustlers, shysters and frauds. He felt, instead, that worst of feelings, the antithesis of capitalist opportunism: genuine empathy. Oh, and what a shame it was! Jajùmissu Cá could have taken this kid for the shirt off his back, had things been different. But as things sat, he couldn't do it. For some reason, he liked Mao. He had a youthful innocence about him that most, J.C. felt, would have lost by his age. J.C. felt like he was face to face with a lost soul, who at this moment was teetering ever so vulnerably between the abyss and the light. And though it might go against everything the Mystic of Mimijad stood for, Jajùmissu Cá, well, J.C. remembered his humble roots. He remembered his years of work and the realization of his lifelong dream to become the Director of the Mimijad Zoo. He had earned that! But mostly, J.C. remembered the words of his wise, dearly departed father:

'Every soul that you destroy is a soul that you become accountable for, in both this life and the next.'

Jajùmissu Cá sighed. His father was right. He had come to terms with his decision. For the first time since donning the fuchsia robe, he would drop the ruse. He would take the hook out, and throw the fish back. The fish might just end up on someone else's line, but he was going to give it a second chance. The fish deserved it.

And so, he broke character, replying not as the Mystic of Mimijad, but instead as himself: Jajùmissu Cá.

"Young man, you seem highly motivated and intelligent. I am sure you will be able to achieve what you set out to do."

"So, is that a yes? You think I have what it takes to write something great, become famous, and be happy?"

Mao's eyes were tinged with desperation. J.C. frowned.

"The truth is that one has absolutely nothing to do with the other, miboy. Happiness is something we pursue from moment to moment. Its nature is fleeting. It is the constant struggle against apathy, and the ease of sliding into cynicism and misery. Happiness is work, miboy. Never forget that. Without work, a man has no purpose. A man must always work for his keep. Keep fighting, keep chasing your ideals, and you will never be lost.

Remember that always, young man, and your chances will be good."

Mao was surprised at the frank, uplifting words the mystic had just spoken. It seemed so... *out of character.* He thought about what the mystic said and it seemed to make sense. He looked into the mystic's earnest eyes, and nodded.

"And what about A–Z? Do you think I can get her back?"

J.C. frowned again.

"You ask the wrong questions, miboy. Get her back, not get her back. That is not important. She will love you, or she will not. That is of little consequence. The question, miboy, is can you get yourself back? Can you learn to let go of all the pain, in order to make room for love again?"

Mao looked over at the shells, as though waiting for them to produce the answer to the mystic's question.

"I'm not sure what you mean. I just want to be happy. Tell me what I need to do."

J.C. shook his head, then reached out to grab Mao's shoulder.

"Look at me."

Mao looked up and met J.C.'s determined gaze.

"I know you don't understand. I didn't understand either at your age. I still don't understand. But tell me, what do you think is the source of happiness?"

Mao considered the question seriously.

"Love? Success? The admiration and respect of my peers?"

J.C. shook his head.

"All of these are good, but they are not the source of happiness, miboy."

"So what is it? Tell me."

Again the voice was tinged with desperation.

J.C. smiled that conspiratorial smile.

"It is simple. The source lies within."

Mao rolled his eyes.

"Oh, c'mon."

J.C. chuckled.

"What is your favorite thing to do, miboy? Aside, of course, from *petting the cat.*"

J.C.'s smile was barely perceptible in the glow of the candlelight. Mao furrowed his brow in thought.

"My favorite thing to do is to write."

J.C. looked over at his neighbor compassionately.

"To write. Are you sure?"

Mao nodded vigorously.

"Yes, I'm sure. I love writing. It is my purpose. I have no doubt."

J.C. inhaled deeply, closed his eyes, and exhaled very slowly. He replied without opening his eyes.

"Good. So write."

Mao raised an eyebrow.

"Write?"

Another deep inhalation, and exhalation.

"Yes. Write."

Mao balled his fists in frustration.

"But I already told you, I can't!"

J.C. remained still.

"Of course you can."

Mao was fidgeting, trying to readjust his position, which had suddenly become uncomfortable.

"I don't know how. I... I can't."

J.C. opened his eyes and looked into Mao's.

"You can't?"

He asked gently.

"No. I can't," Mao replied, defeated.

"I see."

There followed a long silence.

"Couldn't you tell me why? Why can't I write?"

With a placid, content detachment, J.C. replied: "I already have. The source lies within."

Mao grit his teeth. He was getting more and more frustrated with the mystic. Why couldn't he just give him the answer he was looking for? He thought about giving vent to his frustrations, about lashing out at the mystic for his detachment and his seeming disinterest in his paying customer, but then, for some reason, didn't. For some reason, a reason he did not fully understand, Mao said this instead:

"You know, I really idealized A–Z while we were dating. I think that made me view her as a coverall savior figure that was meant to come in and purge me of all my insecurities, frailties, and shortcomings. When that didn't happen, I felt angry. And I thought I was angry with her, but really, I was angry with myself. I was angry with myself for being less than I wanted to be, and I just didn't know how to articulate it. I just didn't understand it. She was never meant to fulfill me. She's just a flawed human, like I am, and it wasn't fair of me to view her as anything more than that. She was my companion, not my savior. There's nothing anyone could do for me that could ever replace what I need to do for myself."

Mao paused. Without even realizing it, tears had begun to stream down his face.

"Why did I act that way? Why was I so stupid?"

J.C. sighed.

"Well, miboy, it's like this. We're all drawn to the comfort of mother's milk. We are all trying to recapture the feeling of sucking at the teat of life. Of feeling safe and secure. Cared for. Taken care of. Some of us fall prey to idealizing the feminine, to maintain the illusion that we could ever recapture that feeling. Some of us prefer other artificial substitutes, whether they be substances, rationalizations, or plain old delusions meant to help us cope with the reality of suffering. But the sad truth is that we cannot go back. The past is gone, and that is just as it is meant to be. You must let go of the notion of recapturing, miboy. Nothing is meant to be recaptured. There is wonder and rebirth in the acceptance of what is, and what is to come. There is beauty to be appreciated in the fleeting nature of life. In the catch as in the release. You cannot crawl back into the womb. None of us can. We must take the world, and all its suffering, as our charge. And we must ride bravely into the night, miboy, or we will not make it through to see the sun rise again."

Mao was taken aback by the poetry in the mystic's words. He wiped his wet, widened eyes, and looked at J.C. as though for the first time.

"But what if..."

"There is no what if!"

J.C. broke in emphatically.

"To 'what if', to doubt, to overthink, that is to be double-minded. To be uncertain is to be divided. And division, miboy, literally means two visions. Two visions: what is and what could be. Two visions breed strife, miboy, and pain. One vision, this is what you strive for. One vision of unity, miboy, and peace. Remember this. Accept what is. Move forward with decisiveness, unity, and purpose, and you will find the harmony that you seek. It is all within you."

Mao let that sit. He took a deep breath, and looked up into the mystic's eyes.

"Mr. Cá, that was beautiful."

J.C. smiled compassionately and then broke into good-natured laughter.

"Yes, well, there's a reason I have a million subscribers on YouTube."

Mao's jaw dropped.

"A million subscribers!?"

J.C. played it cool.

"Focus, miboy."

Mao gathered himself.

"Sometimes, I feel like if I ever really find a way to transcend that longing, then I'll stop being who I am."

J.C. shooed the suggestion away.

"Oh, that's a bunch of rubbish. You can never stop being who you are, miboy. All you need to do is to begin."

The mystic reached into the folds of his habit and produced a large deck of colorful cards tied together with a rubber band. He raised it up to Mao.

"One last thing before our consultation is over. You must draw a card from the tarot. I spent so much time learning the interpretations, miboy, I may as well make good use of all that studying!"

Mao nodded, and J.C. spread the deck facedown on the white mat. He looked at Mao meaningfully, and the latter reached out to draw a card. Mao placed it on the mat, and then turned it over.

"Ah, I knew it," J.C. said thoughtfully.

The card Mao had chosen was the ace of swords.

J.C. laughed heartily, as Mao picked the card up and stared deeply at the illustration of a hand emerging from the clouds, wielding the double-edged sword that pierced, and yet simultaneously held up the golden crown.

"What does it mean?"

Mao asked, with the card still in hand. It somehow felt very powerful.

"It means, miboy, that everything you put your mind to, you will achieve. I have faith in you."

Mao smiled as he thought about everything the mystic said.

Seeing that he had left an impression, the mystic realized that the consultation had come to an end. He stood. Mao, reluctantly, joined him. The mystic led Mao through the maze of candles to the door. Before he opened it, he said: "All the answers you are looking for lie within yourself. I wish you luck on this next chapter of your journey, miboy. You may come and see me again anytime."

Mao looked into the mystic's eccentric face, and reached out a hand. He shook his hand earnestly.

"I hope one day I'll find those answers. At least now, I know where to look. Thank you."

J.C. smiled warmly, and bowed.

"It was my pleasure, miboy."

Mao walked back across the checkered tiles and yellowing walls of the hall into his Apartment #7, and closed the door softly behind him. Leaning on the closed door, and looking deep into the mirror that hung by the front door, he thought: 'That might actually be the best twenty dollars I ever spent.'

XXXII

Excerpt from Mao's Journal
12/01/2020
SUCK IT AND SEE

Of all the Arctic Monkeys records, the only one I could maybe, and that's really only maybe think of as underrated is the provocatively titled, but surprisingly tender Suck it and See. *Although the album is not one of their most popular among fans (I am, of course, speaking relatively – all of the Monkeys' albums are very popular among their fans), I am of the opinion that it features some of Alex Turner's most clever lyricism, and some of his smoothest vocal melodies. The album's composition and production are very clean, and the songs are probably the most pop-oriented in the Monkeys' catalogue. Side One of the record is fun, but I think it's the beautiful songs of longing and heartache on Side Two that, over time, have really stood out to me.*

This was something that she and I always agreed on: that Side Two of Suck it and See *was better than Side One.*

One of the beautiful songs towards the end of the record is the title track, highlighted, for me, by the moment when Turner croons about his love interest's skirt, comparing it to a sawn-off shotgun. I remember the line especially, probably because of the time she asked me about it. We were listening to the record together, in this very apartment, doing nothing in particular when the line came up and I sang it to her in time with the band. I just wanted to be one of the Arctic Monkeys, and so my performance got her to smile, but she stopped me going on to tell me that she didn't get it. I dropped what I was doing (imitating Alex Turner), and set about trying to explain how the comparison of a skirt to a shotgun could serve as a fairly overt metaphor for the use of sex as a weapon, and how Alex Turner's desire to be hit by the 'bullets' was in keeping with his speaker's romantic penchant, which carries throughout the album (as it does throughout so much of his larger body of work). I remember how I waxed poetic on the allure of infatuation, and about how an attraction could be, despite the clear damage it was causing (the figurative shotgun bullets again come to mind), potent enough to entirely eclipse the rational faculty. She was still having a hard time with it, so I teased her about how she had used her shotgun, or cupid's arrow, or feminine guile to get me. I remember expressing how I, like Alex Turner, was glad that she had aimed her weapon at me, and how I was even gladder that she had enough skill to hit me. She thought that was funny - the idea that I was glad she had shot me. I thought it was funny, too.

All the best jokes have a touch of truth in them. And it was true. I was glad. I was glad to have been stricken, glad to have been penetrated so deeply that, even then, it ached. I felt lucky to be experiencing a sensation so real – more real, even, than the everyday emotions I had to make do with before.

So was my romantic penchant.

When she left, I had to re-learn the other reality. The one I had left behind when I openheartedly assumed my place before the firing squad, each penetrating bullet immersing me deeper into the delusion that my reality had become her, and that I was glad it was so. I was angry with her for that. For causing me the inconvenience of growth. My reeling ego wanted desperately to take refuge in the blame. It was, of course, a lot easier to insist that the ball of confusion and anxiety deep inside me was all her fault. It was a long journey to realization, and then another long journey (one that has admittedly not yet been completed, even to this day) to acceptance of the fact that everything inside of me was of my own making.

There's another line on the album I think of often, from the last song 'That's Where You're Wrong'. It is a very simple lyric, about fearing by name and loving by number. That one became infinitely relatable after she left. Because I did fear her, for a long time. I feared what she did to me. What she could still do to me. Her name, for a while, became synonymous with pain. She haunted me, to the point that just the idea of seeing her again was enough to get my heart pumping, and to keep me distracted and preoccupied for hours. It was a favorite pastime of mine, then, to recklessly throw myself into this powerful whirlwind of hypotheticals. To allow myself to be enveloped by the rising tide of emotions.

Though, even the fiercest forces of nature eventually subside.

I feared her by name, but now I am learning to love her by number. Because she is just a person, like any other. Flawed, but inherently good. After her own interests. Trying to find happiness. However she can. In the same way I am just a person, like any other. Flawed, but inherently good. Looking after my own happiness.

I care about her, and always will, because she is a piece of me. I hope she finds what she needs, even though it isn't me. And I am learning to feel this way about her, who I once mistook for everything, because she is a part of me, just like the sun is a part of me, and the moon, and the wind and the trees and all of it. There is a Universe outside of me, of which I am only a part. And there is a Universe within me, of which she was only ever meant to be a part.

The same way nothing external could ever make me whole, nothing external could ever leave me empty.

I've always loved Suck it and See. *Always, since the first time I heard it. It might be my favourite Arctic Monkeys album. And that might just be because I've never felt overly attached to it. It's just always been there, reliably enjoyable and uplifting. And maybe that's the ideal: to feel satisfied with contentment, rather than striving for elation. To be passively accepting of whatever comes my way, and charitable, charitable! Rather than overcome by a desire to control an outcome beyond my control. The counterbalance to euphoria is despair. The counterbalance to holy indifference is only more of the same level-headed contentment.*

Perhaps that is the relationship ideal.

Perhaps that is the lesson I was meant to learn.

The primordial relationship is the one you forge with yourself. Not as an island, no, not at all as an island, but instead as the Universe itself. As a being in its truest form: infinite. Every being is infinite. Every being is one with the Universe within and without it. And when one really stops to think about it, deeply... there comes the chance of eventually coming to the realization that there actually isn't any dividing line between.

XXXIII

Mao walked over to the couch and lay down. He pulled out his smartphone, opened his notes, and wrote something down.

He read it over a few times between long, deep breaths, and then put his phone away. He felt content. He felt at peace.

However, he also felt a faint grumble in his stomach. So, he got up to get an apple from the fridge.

On his way to the kitchen, Mao passed by the spare room and noticed that the door was open.

'That's odd, I was sure I closed it before I went across the hall,' he thought.

Out of curiosity, he stuck his head in, and noticed the two bags of A–Z's things still sitting in the corner of the room.

'I really have to get rid of that crap,' he thought, before turning towards the fridge and the apple.

But then something stopped him in his tracks.

He turned, and for the first time in months, he stepped into the spare room. He grabbed the bags and opened the chain locked door to his apartment. He put his shoes on, then walked through the checkered tiles and yellowing walls of the hall, down the narrow stairwell, through the shabby lobby and out the front door. At the end of the short walkway, he stopped, opened the lid of the trash bin, and threw the bags in. He placed the lid back on top, returned to his apartment, grabbed the apple out of the fridge, sat down on his couch, and ate it with relish.

It was a delicious apple!

But more importantly, beautiful reader, it was a *magic* apple. It had given him the itch. Mao pulled out his phone, and then thought: 'No.' Instead, he opened up his laptop and tried to get comfortable on the couch. Unsurprisingly, he could not. So he went into his spare room, where there was more natural light, and where the desk he was accustomed to working on still lay in its familiar disarray. On the desk, he found more notes in a mess of utter chaos. But for the first time in a long while, he was undeterred.

The flood of ideas, dear reader, had finally come.

Watching the blinker on the blank page, he wrote:

'The future stands on pillars of sand. The past is nebulous; a wisp of smoke. All that is certain is the present moment. It crystallizes before you, whether you embrace it or resist it. To resist divides you from the unavoidable. This division breeds strife, dissatisfaction, and unhappiness. To embrace the present moment is to be one with the universe. To accept whatever comes, and to welcome your fate with open arms. That is the very definition of serenity.'

He took a deep breath.

So, he definitely had an ending in mind... but how would he start it?

'I know! I'll go for a zany angle, and create a narrator that's basically me, but you don't find that out for sure until the end. Yes, I like where this is going,' he thought as his fingers raced across the keys.

'Yes! This can work! "Ah, here we are! We've been expecting you." Yes! I like that, that's pretty funny!'

As his fingers raced across the keys, Mao reflected on everything he had gone through trying to get over A–Z. He thought about how he still missed her sometimes, but now he knew that was okay. He didn't need to self-harm to forget, or to remember. All he needed was to self-love. He needed to be who he was, unapologetically, and let come what may.

"So, have we suffered enough?" he asked aloud to the empty room.

Mao considered the question seriously for a moment, before settling on his answer.

"We all suffer, but I've begun to suspect the name of the game might just be to limit, as best we can, how much of that suffering we cause ourselves."

That brought a smile to Mao's face, and we, unable to contain ourselves, smiled right back.

Finally, old boy, you're starting to sound like a hero!

EPILOGUE

SCENE:

We phase into them in the swing of things.

Nighttime, snowing, a chalet in the woods.

There are four men in the Jacuzzi.

THE BOYS.

The viewer quickly becomes aware that each and every one has already 'taken off'.

Mao is among the ranks, feeling particularly ...::: *emboldened, enlightened, enlivened and thrivin' within the righteous cosmic order, dude* :::... a cigarette in his right hand ...::: *the golden hand* :::... the passing and receiving hand, which he has been deliberately trying to keep ...::: *you cannot smoke a wet* :::... dry, fighting the impulse to ...::: *water is the opposite of fire* :::... join it to his left hand, the hand that is having more fun, all things considered, presently the apex of sensation as it drags and lags, twirls and whirls through the hot, bubbling water in idiosyncratically repeating ...::: *meaning* :::... patterns ...::: *purpose* :::... providing an incomparable sensual delight, as he sits there under the influence of the *moksha*-medicine, which has been reported to serve as a portal to the interconnectedness of all things ...::: *G.O.D.* :::...

Earlier, one of the stoned apes had impishly suggested they 'go to the moon', and the four of them promptly stripped to their boxers and ran out toward the Jacuzzi, which was located along the patio and down the stairs, off to the side of the cottage. They ran out of the chalet, and across the icy deck like children, whooping about in bare feet and knickers, arms overburdened by their determination to make only the one trip with the bottles of wine, and whiskey, the packages of cigarettes, the speaker, the wine glasses, the multiple lighters that only the classy and experienced liberal ...::: *libertine* :::... never leaves behind, and, of course, the several containers ...::: *doobtubes* :::... filled with joints that had been preemptively rolled. ...::: *Rolling is an impossibility once on the bus, of course, as the roads less traveled, indeed the very roads one embarks upon the bus to travel, are always far too turbulent for the origami of rolling* :::...

Above the Jacuzzi, the snow falls gently under a brightly shining full moon, taking its sweet natural time. Beyond the hallowed lights of the cottage, the forest is at rest.
...::: *SOUND* :::...

The large speaker by the Jacuzzi blares.

The Arctic Monkeys' *Tranquility Base Hotel & Casino* is an album, they all agree between large gulps of intoxicants, that must be played 'cover to cover' at maximum volume.

Tonight, Alex Turner serves as guide, serenading the serenely bathing passengers as they make their humble pilgrimage to the moon.

...::: *TIME* :::...

Joints, cigarettes and wine are passed around among the men, while Monkeys lyrics are sung with a verve reserved for the absolutely inimitable feeling of power and pleasure that can only be created through a sensory extravaganza of equal magnitude to a body ninety percent *sous vide* (and to just the right internal temp), ten percent frosted, and married to a mind one hundred percent immersed in the moment unfolding before it. Mao, one observes, is particularly overtaken by the revelation that water droplets are crystalizing to ice on his head, while, one presumes, he puzzles out the paradox that his visible breath in the cold conflicts against the undeniable reality that the rest of his body has never been so comfortable. It is clear that not one of the men has thought for even a second about how the hell he's going to make it back indoors without catching cold, indeed, as the future, as of that moment, remains an illusion nestled within a dubious interpretation of the later-arriving now. And the now Mao finds himself in, the ever-renewing *now*-now, is one among his brothers, accompanied by the sultry, sexy, theatrical musings of a beautiful English madman, the beckoning, mystical glow of a full moon worthy of a mortal's sacrificial howl, and the vital ease of a soul truly at peace.

www.ingramcontent.com/pod-product-compliance
Lightning Source LLC
Chambersburg PA
CBHW071411300726
48976CB00006B/2062